Praise for Maria Grace

"Grace has quickly become one of my favorite authors of Austen-inspired fiction. Her love of Austen's characters and the Regency era shine through in all of her novels." ***Diary of an Eccentric***

"Maria Grace is stunning and emotional, and readers will be blown away by the uniqueness of her plot and characterization" ***Savvy Wit and Verse***

"Maria Grace has once again brought to her readers a delightful, entertaining and sweetly romantic story while using Austen's characters as a launching point for the tale." ***Calico Critic***

"I believe that this is what Maria Grace does best, blend old and new together to create a story that has the framework of Austen and her characters, but contains enough new and exciting content to keep me turning the pages. ... Grace's style is not to be missed." ***From the desk of Kimberly Denny-Ryder***

FROM
Admiration
TO
Love

Maria Grace

White Soup Press

Published by: White Soup Press

From Admiration to Love
Copyright © 2017 Maria Grace

For information, address
author.MariaGrace@gmail.com

ISBN-13: **978-0-9980937-6-5** (White Soup Press)

Author's Website: RandomBitsofFaascination.com
Email address: Author.MariaGrace@gmail.com

Dedication

For my husband and sons.
You have always believed in me.

❧ Chapter 1

A lady's imagination is very rapid; it jumps from admiration to love, from love to matrimony — Jane Austen, *Pride and Prejudice*

Sunday, November 21, 1813

THE VICAR DISMISSED holy services, and Elizabeth filed out of the family pew just behind Darcy. She rubbed her hands over the soft wool of the new navy blue redingote Darcy insisted she order from London—the grey stone of the church did nothing to keep the chill out. She had argued the redingote was an unnecessary expense, but he was right. Derbyshire was definitely colder than she was accustomed to, and all those warm things he bought her would be very welcome indeed.

Darcy had done so many things like that in the

brief year they had been married. He had such a quiet, steady way of taking care of everyone and everything around him, sometimes it was easy to overlook how much he did. But that only proved she had been right when she told Papa he was indeed the best of men.

Georgina and Colonel Fitzwilliam followed as they ducked out of the too-short doorway of the quaint Kympton parish church. Darcy and Fitzwilliam were forever at risk of cracking their heads on the stone lintel. It was old, even as churches went, but it also had character and was filled with characters to appreciate.

The congregants milled just outside the church, enjoying the thin warmth of the late autumn sunshine that shone through skeletal trees, casting dancing shadows on the sandy paths. Though the morning had begun with clouds and fog, it had turned quite pleasant as the sun finally vanquished the gloom. Purple and white passion flowers—blooming a mite late this year—climbed up the church wall, just beside the door. The vines waved in the light breeze that carried the faint scent of the late musk roses growing on the opposite side of the building. Dry leaves crunched under her feet—probably her favorite sound of the season. It made no sense, though, as those same leaves always found a way indoors, to make a mess of her floors and keep the maids constantly sweeping.

"Mr. Darcy?" One of the major tenant farmers approached with a small bow. Mr. Rowley was a round, red-faced man, with eight strapping sons who now did most of the work of the farm. He had the look of a man who was perpetually on the verge of losing his temper, but was in fact, quite pleasant. His eldest son's banns were read this morning. The wedding would be in just a few weeks. Mr. Rowley hoped to secure the lease of one of the neighboring farms for his son. No doubt he wished to continue the discussion now.

Elizabeth curtsied and wandered toward Georgiana who stood in a small knot of girls close to her age. It was only in the last year that she had begun to make friends in the neighborhood. Darcy had said she had shown no interest before. Of course, she said she had no interest when she had no opportunity to interact with the local girls during morning calls or visits. Once Elizabeth began paying calls and bringing Georgiana with her, suddenly the dear child was making friends with aplomb. Amazing that.

"Good morning, Mrs. Darcy," Miss Sarah Hawkesbury curtsied, very prettily and a mite more deeply than necessary. The pale, freckled girl always seemed a bit too in awe of Elizabeth, almost an exact opposite of Lydia in all possible ways, but she was a sweet girl and easy to like.

Beside her Miss Florence Roberts and Miss Emilia Millington dipped and bowed their heads. Miss Roberts' mother was Italian by birth. She favored her mother, with dark eyes and olive skin, and a vivacious personality that had the unfortunate tendency to overshadow all the other girls in the room. Miss Millington had an annoying propensity to giggle whenever she was addressed. Sadly, it made her appear vapid and silly when in fact she had a very intelligent and lively mind.

"My mother has asked me to thank you again for inviting us to your Twelfth Night ball. We are excited to be there for Miss Darcy's come out." Though she attempted to be grown-up now that she was out, Miss

Roberts' smile was still that of an excited little girl.

Georgiana blushed bright. Poor dear was still not comfortable with the idea of coming out at the ball. Though Elizabeth had been slowly warming her into it by bringing her on calls and hosting numerous small parties at Pemberley, she was still reluctant. Only when Elizabeth promised that her just-now-out friends could attend did she finally acquiesce.

Mama, had she known, would be horrified at the notion of inviting anyone who might take attention away from "dear Miss Darcy." Truly, it was unlikely. Though gentlewomen, none of the other girls could rival Georgiana's fortune or connections, making them hardly rivals at all. Fortunately, they all knew it, but they largely ignored the matter in favor of enjoying their friendship. More importantly, the girls' mothers understood and did not appear to be trying to push their daughters to take advantage of their connection to Georgiana.

Gracious, how complicated society could be!

"We are very glad you all will be able to join us. It has been a long time since Pemberley has hosted a Twelfth Night ball. We hope this one will be quite memorable." Elizabeth caught Georgiana's eye, hopefully with a look of encouragement.

"Have you decided on what fancy dress you will wear?" Miss Millington tittered.

"One of Shakespeare's fairies, I think." Georgiana glanced at Elizabeth for approval.

Elizabeth smiled and nodded. How long it had taken to settle on that idea!

"Oh! You shall be so beautiful, no doubt. You are so lithe. You will be a perfect fairy!" Miss Roberts gushed. "Mama has said I should be a Spanish infanta…"

Elizabeth smiled and turned aside. The girls had been debating fancy dress since they first heard of the ball and would probably still be talking about it at Easter. Still, it was an innocent enough diversion, leaving them merry as girls their age should be.

Fitzwilliam stood off with several of the gentlemen of the neighborhood, but he was not attending to the conversation. That vaguely dissatisfied, vaguely lonely expression he wore when he thought no one was looking crept upon him. He would never admit it, but the way he often needled Darcy about being a settled, married man suggested Fitzwilliam was envious of the state and would not mind a few careful introductions made on his behalf. Generally matchmaking was to be avoided, but when a man all but asked for it, was not a little assistance appropriate?

There were one or two young ladies in the neighborhood whose fortunes and temperaments fit what Fitzwilliam required. What was more, they had been on the ball's guest list since before Fitzwilliam arrived. So no machinations were necessary. The introductions would flow naturally. Who could object to that?

Darcy approached and offered his arm. "Fitzwilliam said he would escort Georgiana back to the house. Shall we go?"

She slipped her hand in the crook of his elbow. "Yes. I should like to have a little time to prepare the makings of the Christmas pudding before they arrive."

"You are still determined to have a traditional Stir It Up Sunday? You have been so tired—"

"Indeed I am. Pemberley has been too long without proper Christmas celebrations, and I intend to rectify that."

"Are you suggesting last year—" Darcy cocked his head and lifted an eyebrow. Teasing man!

"I had only been Mistress of Pemberley a se'nnight before Christmastide began. There was hardly time to plan anything at all. And with Lady Matlock—"

He grumbled under his breath. "Pray do not remind me of all her kind assistance. I still have not quite forgiven her for the part she played in your sprained ankle. I do not take seeing you hurt lightly."

"I agree, she was less than helpful. But, the fall was my own fault. I do not intend to repeat it. This year my plans are all made well in advance, and there will be no misunderstandings at all."

"I would settle for no injuries."

"That is in my plans as well."

"Then I shall hold you to them." He pressed his hand over hers.

So dear and protective he was.

"Of course you will. What news did you have for Mr. Rowley?"

AFTER A LIGHT nuncheon, Elizabeth invited Darcy, Georgiana, and Fitzwilliam to the kitchen, just as her mother had done every Stir it Up Sunday since Elizabeth could remember. Pemberley's kitchen was huge compared to Longbourn's, filled with servants baking, making plum puddings, and working on dinner preparations. The air was thick with the fragrances of brandy and spices hanging in the humid heat of the great boiling cauldrons already containing prepared puddings. How many were needed to distribute on the estate and in the parish? Elizabeth had lost count. Thankfully Cook had not.

A worktable had been set up in a more-or-less out of the way corner of the kitchen, with all the sweet-smelling makings for plum pudding ready and waiting in small bowls. The menfolk would have no patience for chopping and measuring, so it was best done for them. Even this was a little too much like cooking for their comfort. She gestured for them to stand around the table.

"I do hope you are going to tell us what to do." Fitzwilliam laughed and elbowed Darcy.

"What, you do not know how to cook, too?" Elizabeth reached for the large earthenware bowl in the middle of the table. "You would have me believe an officer of His Majesty—albeit former officer—capable of anything."

"I can roast a haunch of meat over a campfire, if that is what you are asking. But more than that I am told is not the province of men."

"But are not French man-cooks considered the height of culinary expression?" Georgiana stared at the table. She had grown far more bold and able to tease—and be teased—good-naturedly, but still was not fully sure of herself in doing it.

"I stand corrected." Fitzwilliam bowed at Georgiana. "I shall immediately find myself an apprenticeship with one of them and shower you with fine offerings from the kitchen."

Georgiana giggled.

"I would be pleased if you would simply bring back some venison when you go hunting." Elizabeth lifted her brows and stared at him.

Fitzwilliam laughed heartily.

"Perhaps we ought to attend to the pudding?" Darcy struggled not to smile.

"A very good suggestion indeed. Now, we have thirteen ingredients to add—"

"A most auspicious number, thirteen. I am told it is unlucky." Fitzwilliam peered at the small bowls on the table and counted under his breath.

"Thirteen for Christ and the apostles." Elizabeth drummed her fingers on the table. "Has your mother not taught you—"

"My mother had nothing to do with the kitchen, even for the sake of a Christmas pudding, unlike Aunt Darcy who was quite as fond of stirring them up as you. You, my dear cousin, must make up for my mother's lack."

"Then pay attention, or I shall have to send you out like a recalcitrant school boy, and have our master deal with you." Elizabeth gestured toward Darcy.

Darcy snorted. Poor man might hurt himself trying to keep a straight face.

"A dire threat indeed. I shall behave myself with all decorum now." Fitzwilliam raised open hands in surrender.

"See that you do. Now, I shall add the flour and suet and pass it to the east." She pushed the bowl toward Fitzwilliam. "You have the dried fruits and nuts—just pour them in on top, like that. You might make a man-cook yet."

Fitzwilliam lifted his hand high and sprinkled in the chopped nuts with a flourish, then passed the bowl to Georgiana.

"Add in the bread crumbs and milk. Here is the citron already soaked in brandy. Pour that in, too."

"You have kept the brandy from me?" Fitzwilliam wrinkled his face into a pout.

"My wife is very wise in all things." Darcy took the bowl from Georgiana. He poured in the spices, eggs and sugar from the small bowls near him.

"And you my dear are the most sensible of men." Elizabeth took the bowl again and reached for a wooden spoon. "This spoon is to remind us of the wood of the Christ child's crib. Now stir it clockwise with your eyes closed and make a wish."

"That is a relief, I thought you might hit me with that." Fitzwilliam took the spoon.

"I will have to keep that possibility in mind. Now, stir the pudding."

"By Jove, this is heavy! I had no idea!" He struggled to pull the spoon through the pudding.

Georgiana crowded him away from the bowl. "Here, here, stop complaining, and let me." She struggled against the heavy batter.

"Stir up, we beseech thee, the pudding in the pot. And when we do get home tonight, we'll eat it up hot." Fitzwilliam crossed his arms and pressed his tongue into his cheek. "Or not, at the rate you are going."

"Help me, brother." Georgiana handed Darcy the spoon.

Cradling the bowl with one arm, he dragged the spoon through the thick slurry. A fine sheen of sweat broke out on his forehead. "I think I do not pay our cook enough."

Fitzwilliam slapped his thighs and chortled.

"Is it done now, Elizabeth?" Georgiana asked.

"Only one more thing to add." She took the bowl from Darcy. "We cannot forget the charms! They are very dear to my family. You see, each year when someone has found the ring, they have indeed become betrothed. It began with my mother and father."

"Did you find the ring the year my brother offered you marriage?"

"No, but the husband of one of my sisters did, so the tradition continued." No need to mention it was Wickham who found the ring that year. She dropped the silver charms into the pudding and stirred until they disappeared amidst the dried fruits and nuts, and she was quite short of breath. "Georgiana, hand me that buttered cloth, and you two strong gentlemen— who do not pay the cook enough for this chore— dump out the pudding and tie it up to boil."

Darcy and Fitzwilliam struggled with the pudding, finally calling in Cook's assistance to tie it up and haul it away to a large boiling cauldron.

"With that, I think I shall seek out some far easier recreation. What say you Georgiana, would archery suit you?" Fitzwilliam mimicked drawing a bow.

"You consider that easier than making a pudding?"

"Far easier and cleaner." He dusted flour off his jacket. "Shall we have a quarter of an hour to clean the flour from our hands and don our shooting dress? I will see you on the back lawn then?"

"I am a frightful bad shot you know." Georgiana followed him out.

"Not an incurable malady I assure you."

Darcy shook his head as he watched them leave, then turned his gaze on Elizabeth. "You have flour on your cheek."

"Do I?"

He pulled out his handkerchief and dusted her

cheek, gently, tenderly, almost like a kiss. "There, much better."

"I am certain this is not the way your mother must have stirred up puddings." She bit her lower lip.

"What matter is that? Pemberley needs laughter, and I am thankful to hear it. I look forward to many more Christmas puddings stirred up just this way."

She leaned her head on his shoulder. "I am glad to hear that."

"There is one favor I might ask, though. Is there any way to prevent that ring from finding its way into either Fitzwilliam's or Georgiana's pudding? I can see no good coming of it, especially in the presence of a large party."

"You mean this one?" She opened her hand. A tiny silver ring twinkled in the sunlight.

"My wife is indeed the wisest woman in Derbyshire!"

"Not in all of England?"

"I am not far from being convinced of that as well."

❧ Chapter 2

December 6, 1813

DARCY PEEKED OVER his newspaper. Elizabeth sat across the morning room table in a happy sunbeam. The sky blue walls, white, wispy curtains and the vaseful of French marigolds from the garden made it easy to imagine she was sitting somewhere in the gardens she so loved.

She was absorbed in her sewing—what was that she was making? Another baby dress for the parish, no doubt. There had been so many babies born this year, it seemed like she was constantly sewing them.

Pemberley had an outstanding mistress in her. Mother would have been proud. She even looked just the tiniest bit like Mother, sitting in mother's favorite spot in the room, where the light was best for sewing.

The house ran smoothly under Elizabeth's administration and, after a bit of settling in, the local matrons came to respect her even as the parish looked to her for guidance. She had been a little daunted at first, but who would not be? Even so, she had done him proud. But perhaps she was working too hard, though. She seemed tired so often, even if she never complained.

She turned slightly toward him and lifted her eyebrow. He was staring again. He chuckled and turned his eyes back to his newspaper. Technically, staring was a bit rude, but with such an object for his attention, who could blame him? At least she took it in good humor.

Marriage—to the right woman—was a very, very good thing.

He sipped his coffee and savored the cinnamon in the air, wafting from the plate of warm Chelsea buns Mrs. Reynolds had just brought in. There was nothing to compare to Pemberley's Chelsea buns, sweet and spicy, full of currants and sticky with sugar glaze—he licked his lips.

"Mr. Darcy!" Mrs. Reynolds dashed into the room breathless and a little wild-eyed.

Elizabeth jumped to her feet, her sewing slipping to the floor. "What has happened?"

"Callers ... I mean guests ... pray forgive me but the house is not ready. We had no idea ..."

Darcy folded his paper and set it aside. "Who has come? We are not expecting anyone."

"Pray tell me Lydia and her ... husband ... they have not arrived on our doorstep, have they?" Elizabeth clutched the back of her chair almost as though dizzy.

Darcy gritted his teeth. There was one person who was definitely not welcome under his roof, and unfortunately it was his sister's husband. Denying him succor would be very awkward indeed, especially at Christmastide, but no one could reasonably expect him to be tolerated when Georgiana was resident in the house.

"No, Mrs. Darcy, not them. It is Lady Catherine and Miss de Bourgh!"

Elizabeth's jaw dropped. "You did not tell me you invited her."

"I did no such thing! I have no idea why they are here."

"Lady Catherine is waiting for you in your study, sir. I am sorry, but she would not be stopped. Miss de Bourgh is in the ladies' parlor. She did not say, but if I may be so forward, it seems that she would speak with you, Mrs. Darcy." Mrs. Reynolds wrung her hands in her apron.

"Have refreshments sent to both of them, and see that the maids make up rooms for them in the family wing—the far side of the family wing." Elizabeth glanced at Darcy.

"I suppose there is little else to do. Tell Lady Catherine that I will be with her shortly. I will have my breakfast first."

Mrs. Reynolds shuffled away, still wringing her hands. Aunt Catherine had a way of terrorizing the staff wherever she went. Elizabeth turned to him with a very peculiar look in her eye—she was rarely caught off guard and apparently did not appreciate it.

"I am going to enjoy my buns. There is every chance that I will be in no mood to eat once I have finished with Aunt Catherine, and I will not allow

Cook's efforts to go to waste." He reached for a warm sticky bun and took a generous bite. "Not to mention you have not had your gift yet."

"My what?" She retrieved her sewing from the floor and folded it into her sewing basket.

"It was a tradition between my parents to exchange a small gift on St. Nicholas Day."

"Why did you not tell me? I—"

"I suppose I should have, but I have been selfish this year. I wanted to have the privilege to myself just once." He rose and opened a drawer in the sideboard, withdrawing a slim package wrapped in brown paper. "The Gardiners helped me with this, so I trust it will be to your liking."

Her eyes glittered, and she smiled: a little shy, a little delighted. Did she realize what a gift that was—to be so pleased with him?

She untied the string and unfolded the paper to reveal the blue, purple and gold silk beneath. Gasping, she held it up. The fabric cascaded from her hands to the floor, shimmering in the morning sun.

"You have spent so much time on Georgiana's fancy dress for the ball. I thought you should have something equally special. It is a saree, from India. Your aunt will write to you with instructions on how to wear it. After the ball, if you like, you might have it made into an evening gown."

She wrapped the saree across her chest and stared down at it. "The colors, the fabric, it is so beautiful." She twirled in the nearest sunbeam. "I am glad Aunt Gardiner has instructions for this. I have no idea what to do with so much fabric!"

"I have seen them worn. It will suit you very well."

She returned the saree to its wrapping. "You are so

dear to think of such a thing—truly you spoil me. I had not given a thought to—"

"Exactly, my dearest." He stood and drew her very close. "You do so much for all of Pemberley. It is a gift to be able to do something for you." He leaned down; a kiss was definitely in order.

"Ah… Mr. Darcy…" Why did Mrs. Reynolds have to come in now? "Excuse me, sir. Lady Catherine is growing most restive."

"I will be there, Mrs. Reynolds. You are dismissed." So much for not growling at the staff. "Now where was I?"

Elizabeth stood on tiptoes and pressed her lips to his, warm and soft and entirely too suggestive for so early in the day, especially with company waiting. Her eyes met his, twinkling a promise that just might sustain him through what was to come.

He kissed her once more, finished his Chelsea bun and steeled himself for his unexpected company.

"I will see to Anne," she called after him. "Perhaps, between their stories, we can get a true picture of what has brought them to Pemberley."

He nodded, but did not look back lest he roll his eyes at her which, he was told, most considered rude.

His fingers were still sticky, so he paused at the study door to wipe them on his handkerchief, straighten his jacket—and dab away beads of sweat on his forehead. There was no reason Aunt Catherine should instill such a reaction in him. But those boyhood recollections were hard to shake away. Father had visited Rosings every Easter and had brought him along. Aunt Catherine was not particularly tolerant of the childhood adventures he and Fitzwilliam—and on rare occasions Anne—had shared.

Drawing a deep breath, he strode into his study.

Aunt Catherine paced along the windows, staring out into the neat fields in the distance. Her skirt rustled against the nearby chairs and tables placed not quite far enough away from the windows to allow her full, old-fashioned skirts to pass unimpeded. He stood in front of his neat walnut desk, flanked by an impressive bookcase and waited for her to acknowledge him.

She crossed back and forth along the windows three more times before finally noticing him from the corner of her eye. "Why did you keep me waiting?"

"Why have you arrived without any invitation or even a letter announcing you would come?"

"Am I not family? Do you suggest that I am not welcome?" She bristled, like an angry hen puffing her feathers.

"Is it not customary to announce a visit before it is made, particularly during the holiday season when I might be accommodating other guests?"

"Your housekeeper says you are only hosting Fitzwilliam and are having no other guests arriving this season."

"That is not the point. Does not etiquette require—"

She whirled on him. "Etiquette be damned!"

He staggered back and leaned on his desk. "Excuse me?"

"You heard me very well." She stomped toward him. "This is no time to be concerned about etiquette. I am dealing with a crisis—an emergency, and I need your help."

"An emergency?"

"Yes, an emergency, and I do not know where else

to turn."

"Have you told Uncle Matlock? I am certain he is able—"

"No I have not talked to my brother. He is as much a problem as what I am dealing with."

"I know you have had your disagreements in the past—"

"That is hardly the word for it. I am not speaking to him. All he does is shove Fitzwilliam at me, and that is hardly any help at all." She pressed her hands to the sides of her face.

"Pray sit down." He led the way to a pair of chairs near the window. "Now, explain, completely and in detail, what you are talking about."

"He insists that Fitzwilliam should marry Anne since you did not do your duty by her."

He grumbled under his breath. "If you have come to berate me on my choice of wife, I will have your coach brought around immediately."

She flung her hands in the air, gesticulating wildly. "What is done is done, and I cannot change that now. But that does not mean that Anne should settle for … for …"

"The well-connected son of an earl?"

"A man whose wealth is not equal to her own."

So that was Aunt Catherine's prejudice against him. She had never actually voiced it to him before. "What has Anne's non-existent husband to do with any of this?"

"The de Bourghs are coming."

The study door swung open, and Fitzwilliam saun-tered in. "Morning Darcy, Mrs. Reynolds told me the most extraordinary thing, that Aunt Cath…"

Aunt Catherine rose. "Good morning, nephew."

Fitzwilliam skittered back several steps, blinking rapidly. Apparently he shared Darcy's childhood recollections. "Aunt? I did not know you were expected."

"She was not." Darcy gestured to a nearby chair. "Join us. It seems Aunt Catherine is in need of some assistance."

Fitzwilliam hurried to take a seat. "What is wrong?"

She worked her teeth over her upper lip, eyes narrowing. "The de Bourghs are coming."

"You said that already, but I still have no idea what you are talking about. You make it sounds as though the French are massing on the border." Darcy raked his hair. Why did Aunt Catherine always leave him doing that?

"The de Bourghs, my late husband's family. They are coming to Rosings."

"And the problem with that is?" Fitzwilliam asked.

"Fool! Can you not see?" She leaned across to slap Fitzwilliam's knee. "They want Rosings Park."

Fitzwilliam donned a patient smile that meant he was anything but. "Rosings belongs to Anne."

"Of course it does. But they want it. They are offended that she inherited it—claim the estate should have been entailed to keep it in the de Bourgh line. They are sending eligible de Bourgh men to try and seduce Anne into marrying one of them to bring it back into the family!"

Fitzwilliam snickered. "Seduce Anne? I hardly think that possible. She has always done what you have told her, why do you think that will change?"

She turned and waggled a finger at Darcy. "That we can thank Darcy for. You are responsible for this calamity, so you must remedy it."

Darcy rubbed his eyes with thumb and forefinger. "How exactly is that?"

"After you failed to marry her, I decided to send her away to school for a year, to refine her accomplishments—"

"To prepare her for the marriage mart," Fitzwilliam muttered under his breath.

Aunt Catherine glowered at him. "She needed some small bit of tutoring to polish—"

"Forgive me, but Anne lacks—or at least lacked— the most basic accomplishments of a lady in society. She cannot play or sing, can hardly dance. She speaks no language but English, when she chooses to speak at all. Even her manners are highly questionable." Darcy looked to Fitzwilliam as though seeking confirmation.

"How dare you criticize my daughter! Besides, she has other allurements."

"You speak of Rosings Park, which is why the de Bourghs are sending suitors for her." Fitzwilliam rose and stomped to the window, his back toward them. "She can be easily and suitably married to any of them, and your problem is solved. I believe there is even a title or two among the family, which should be quite to your liking. I do not see what your concern is."

"Of course not. I did not expect you to be of much help." She slapped the arms of her chair and focused on Darcy. "In the first place, that foul seminary in Bath has turned Anne into a wild sort of … of romping girl that I hardly understand! She is disrespectful and disobedient. I barely recognize her as my daughter. She tried to order me to the dower house last week! Can you imagine?"

Fitzwilliam coughed—a hardly effective attempt at concealing a snicker.

Aunt Catherine's eyes narrowed into narrow, dark slits. Was that the expression Medusa had used to turn her enemies into stone? "All that aside, there is no way, absolutely none, that I will permit the de Bourghs to get their hands on Rosings Park again. That is my final word on the matter."

"Anne is of age. Technically, you have no word on the matter," Fitzwilliam muttered to the window.

"She will do as I say. You will see to that. That is your duty, Darcy." She met his gaze with a frighteningly determined one of her own.

"What do you have against the de Bourghs? All propriety would suggest it right for the estate to remain in their line, that the family was materially harmed when it went to Anne. If she were to actually like one of these de Bourgh fellows enough to marry him, why would that be so bad?

"Because he would be a de Bourgh, and they are all alike. I was married to one. No daughter of mine will ever be."

Fitzwilliam turned and caught Darcy's eye with an upraised eyebrow.

FITZWILLIAM LEANED BACK in his chair and listened as Aunt Catherine talked around the same points for nearly an hour. She never really added anything of substance, just got louder and more adamant with each repetition. Darcy's looks pleaded for help several times, but nothing Fitzwilliam could say would improve the situation. Long ago Aunt Catherine had decided he was as superfluous as his family thought he was—the heir was hale and hearty, so what need was there for the spare? Darcy though, his opinions were important, he had weight in the family.

By all rights, Fitzwilliam could, and perhaps even should be jealous. But there was a great deal of work and unpleasantness involved in that. Much better to find equanimity in other ways, like maintaining a clandestine friendship with Anne while none of the rest of the family were the wiser for it.

Finally, Aunt Catherine trundled off in a cloud of taffeta and offense, to be led to her quarters by the long-suffering Mrs. Reynolds. As soon as the door shut, Fitzwilliam plucked a key from Darcy's desk and hurried to unlock a pair of doors in a nearby cabinet revealing a crystal decanter and glasses. He poured two glasses of brandy and returned to Darcy.

"Do not try to talk until you have had a sip or four. It is far too early in the season to allow her to give you an apoplexy."

Darcy grunted and sipped his brandy. "Anne at school? I had no idea. What could she be thinking, sending Anne to a finishing school at her age?"

Fitzwilliam ran his tongue along his lower teeth. "She mentioned it to me, shortly after your marriage—she was quite in high dudgeon at the time, and I hardly thought her serious. But for the record, I did tell her I thought it a very bad idea."

"Which probably made her all the more determined to do it." Darcy rolled his eyes.

"Of course. Can you imagine how humiliating it must have been, to be so much older than the rest of the students there? Do you suppose Aunt Catherine lied about Anne's age?" Was it wrong to pretend that he knew nothing of this when he and Anne had discussed it at length the last time he had been in Bath?

"It would not surprise me if she had, to try to save face." Darcy dragged his hand over his face. "Have you any idea what she has against the de Bourghs?"

"While I tend to know far more than most of the family would like for me to, I have no idea."

"Shall I write to your father to see if he knows anything, or—"

"If he knows anything, it will be you he tells, not me." Fitzwilliam's lip curled back just a mite. Anne, on the other hand, might just be very willing to tell him as soon as he could get a moment alone with her to ask. All of this was very peculiar, even more so than things usually were when Anne was involved.

ELIZABETH PAUSED AT the parlor door. Dealing with Lydia and Kitty, even Mary was one thing, but Anne was no younger sister. She was five years older than Elizabeth, and according to Darcy, quite as proud as her mother. Would she consider Elizabeth her peer? Did she really wish to talk as Mrs. Reynolds suggested? She never had in all the time Elizabeth had spent in Kent both before and after she had become Mrs. Darcy. More likely, Anne intended to try to order her about as Lady Catherine did. That would not do, not at Pemberley.

Elizabeth drew a deep breath. None of this line of thinking was doing her any good. Best get this over with. She smoothed her skirt and strode into the neat little ivory parlor where she entertained local ladies when they called. The furniture was light and dainty, upholstered in pale blue florals over ivory painted wood. Matching curtains were tied back from the tall windows that overlooked the informal flower garden. Tall vases with sunflowers and poppies added color and guided the eye from the curio cabinet in one corner to the plinky old harpsichord that Elizabeth refused to remove from the opposite corner. If nothing else, it was a good source for conversation when topics ran sparse.

Anne stood at the far end of the room, in front of the bookcase. She jumped a little as the door squeaked, and turned to face Elizabeth, a rather large book in her hand. Tall, like her mother, her figure was columnar and elegant, in an ordinary sort of way despite the fine white muslin that draped it. Her face was pretty and plain at the same time. Really, there was very little to recommend her as any great beauty. Still though, there was a spark in her features that Elizabeth had never seen before, enough to be intriguing. What had happened to put it there?

"I have heard this novel is quite entertaining, have you read it?" Anne asked mildly, as though there was nothing odd happening at all.

Elizabeth stepped to the middle of the room. "I started reading it, but found I could not like the heroine at all. She became insipid in the second volume."

Anne replaced the book on the shelf. "Then, it is not for me. I have no use for insipid. Do you have one you might recommend? I may be here a very long time, and I might as well have some reliable form of entertainment."

So this was how it would be? And she intended to extend her stay for quite some time? What was she, a prisoner seeking asylum?

"I am sorry you do not think Pemberley will be up

to entertaining you, Miss de Bourgh. If you do not feel it will be to your liking, you are free to return to Rosings. I will take no offense. We tend to be a quiet, family party most of the time. You might find us very dull indeed."

Anne threw her head back and laughed heartily, a decidedly odd, screechy sound that resembled a hinge that needed oiling. "You will do very well indeed! I cannot think how it was Darcy managed to convince you to marry him; he is such a dry, dull sort. You of course already know. But he seems to have chosen very well for himself."

Elizabeth's jaw dropped. Who was this woman who looked so much like Anne de Bourgh, but sounded and behaved nothing like her?

"You do not know what to make of me? Good. I like that." Anne claimed the largest chair in the room and settled upon it like a throne.

"I am pleased you have found something here to your liking." Elizabeth tried not to roll her eyes as she sat across from Anne. She probably ought to moderate her tone, too. A lady did not express irritation to her guests, even uninvited—and probably unwelcome—ones.

"Oh, do not be that way, Elizabeth. Pray, do not. I cannot have done that much to offend you, not so soon in my stay." She folded her hands before her chest, so prim and proper.

"It does not seem you have gone out of your way to be agreeable either." Gracious! That was curt. Elizabeth pinched her temples. Lydia had been equally trying, and she had managed to find the patience to deal with her. Surely she could do it now.

Anne laughed again, but without any trace of bitterness. "You are very direct—Darcy must have taught you that as no mother in England would ever permit her daughter to be so. You must wonder why I have come."

"The thought did cross my mind."

"Of course it did, with us showing up here with no warning, my mother shrieking like a banshee and demanding an audience with Darcy."

"Excuse me?"

"Oh, you heard me correctly." Anne smiled—no grinned—as though she was heartily enjoying Elizabeth's discomfort. "I know well what my mother is like. I have lived with her all my life, well except for the last year in Bath at the seminary. Truly the best year I have ever spent. I cannot recommend it highly enough for any young woman."

"You have been away at school? Did not Lady Catherine always decry sending young ladies away from home as irresponsible and unnecessary? Besides, I thought your health was too delicate to allow you to travel."

"I heard that for years, until Mother decided that I needed polishing since Darcy did not 'do his duty to the family' and marry me. She thought somehow the experience would make me more agreeable to some gentlemen so that I might be a proper married woman and get an heir for Rosings Park."

"I see. Is she as pleased as you are with the results?"

Anne chewed her cheek and flashed her eyebrows. "Mother is not well pleased. She is convinced that I am totally gone wild. And perhaps I have."

At some point soon, she needed to ask the name of the establishment Anne attended. Under no circumstances would Georgiana—or any Darcy child—be permitted to set foot in the place.

"Upon further reflection though, I do not think it the case, as I have only just begun to express what I have always been." Anne sniggered. "You find that shocking?"

"I am surprised to be sure. You have never taken the opportunity to speak to me in the past. I do not believe I have ever heard you put more than two sentences together at any one time."

"Entirely true, right and fair. It was not until I went to Bath that I experienced the delight of actually being heard. You see at home, mother did all the talking—a very great deal of it, and ensured that no one else was heard. After decades of that, can you blame me for giving up and not bothering?"

"I suppose not." That was largely how she, Jane and Mary had coped with Lydia.

"I allowed her to find satisfaction in that way, I had mine in others. It is quite a delight to secretly vex her you know." Anne leaned forward and dropped her voice to nearly a whisper. "To this day she believes that all my governesses were truly worthless wretches who taught me nothing. That I cannot sing or play or dance, much less speak on any matter."

"I often heard that mentioned in after-dinner conversation."

"I know. Have you forgotten, I was there as well? Are you surprised to learn, my mother is entirely wrong? I am actually very good at all those things and learned from all those dreadful women she employed to teach me. I just chose not to show any of them my accomplishments. Why should I if she would not give me the courtesy of hearing what I had to say? At the seminary in Bath though, it was quite a different story. I was quite the pet of the school, so accomplished was I, the star pupil for acquiring such a high level of proficiency so very quickly." Anne clasped her hands before her and flashed a very false smile.

"So, why have you left school when you found it so very agreeable?"

"Mother of course. Well, she and the headmistress. They decided it was best that I should go after they learned that I had acquired suitors at the school." Anne giggled behind her hand.

"Suitors?" Elizabeth gulped.

"Yes, three of them, in fact. More than any other girl at the school had. And mine were gentlemen, *bona fide* not just dandies playing at being gentlemen."

"And were you able to confirm that these gentlemen were who they claimed to be?"

"They were known to one of my school chums. Moreover, they vouched for one another. I would think that they would have every reason to discredit one another, since they are all trying for the same prize." She batted her eyes.

If she did that when her suitors were present, it was a wonder they persisted.

"Would your mother have approved any of these so-called gentlemen?"

"She never approves anything I want or like and never has. They would be no different, particularly since none of them would be apt to listen to her. She would have me marry some wealthy puppy who would kowtow to her just as she had me doing all my life. I have only just begun to live. Do you think I could possibly want to return to her complete control?" Anne's voice rose to nearly a shriek.

"I do not imagine it would be appealing."

"Hardly, hardly at all. I will not do it. Not for her, not for anyone. She dragged us here because she hopes Darcy will bring me under 'proper regulation' as she calls it. But, I cannot imagine he will. He married you, after all, defying my mother entirely. If anything, I would think he would support me to do as he did. Perhaps, if you and Darcy supported me, then Mother would not be so set against me. I might continue to see my suitors and choose a husband for myself, without interference from her. Is that not what you both did?"

"I suppose so, after a fashion. But Lady Catherine is not Darcy's mother and my parents did not object to him. And, to be perfectly honest, my position was very different to your own. I did not bring an estate into our marriage as you will. I have seen what a foolish, spendthrift husband can do to a woman—a sister—and it is worse than you might imagine. I pray you do not make a foolish choice. You are far more vulnerable than you understand. Rich young ladies like you and Georgiana must be very careful and examine the character of any man who pays you attention. You are in a position to lose very much indeed."

Anne rose and stamped her foot. "You sound just like my mother! I had thought you would be on my side, that you would help me!"

"I ... we will, you can be sure of that. At the same time though, we do not want to see you hurt."

"You do not want to see me happy!" Anne balled her fists and shook them at her sides. Lady Catherine had done that same thing when she had visited Elizabeth at Longbourn—was it only a little over a year ago?

"Of course we do, but happiness—"

"I do not need another lecture. I do not want to hear it, and I will not. I simply will not. I am tired and will go to my rooms now!" She tossed her head and marched out of the parlor.

Hopefully her chambers would be ready, or Mrs. Reynolds would be privy to a memorable temper tantrum.

Was this girl truly Anne de Bourgh? And if she was, what were they going to do with her?

℘Chapter 3

FITZWILLIAM LEANED BACK and sipped his wine, watching the players at the dining table over the rim of his glass. The small dining room felt especially full tonight, even though there were only six in attendance. The table would comfortably seat eight, maybe even ten if they were the size of Georgiana. Darcy and Elizabeth sat opposite each other, exchanging glances that they probably thought private, but shouted their discomfort quite clearly, even if no one else chose to notice.

Filled with candles that glittered off mirrors and crystal, and garden flowers for color, the dining room was all that was comfortable and inviting, at least as much as when Aunt Darcy had been alive, maybe even more so. The table held a wide array of dishes, offering a bounty of mouthwatering scents. The generous spread was a particular testament to Elizabeth's management, considering only a simple family dinner had been planned prior to Aunt Catherine's invasion. But that was only the opinion of a coarse, uninformed soldier—one who had grown up in an earl's home run by a countess known throughout England for her hospitality. What should he know on the matter?

Aunt Catherine took rather a large gulp of wine. That was not a good sign. Usually it presaged a diatribe. "I confess, I am rather shocked not to see any venison on the table, Mrs. Darcy."

Elizabeth opened her mouth, but Fitzwilliam cut her off. "You may blame me for the absence, aunt. I have been rather off my shot recently. We have had brutish luck hunting these last weeks. Darcy is an excellent enough host that he does not want to show me up in front of the ladies."

Anne tittered and whispered something to Georgiana that left the poor girl stammering and blushing. Darcy glowered, but it probably was not a bad thing to accustom Georgiana to the outrageous things that commonly happened amongst 'better' company.

Odd how it seemed the higher ranking the company, the more outlandish the things that might happen. Still though, it was difficult when it was one's own family proving outlandish.

Darcy glared first at Anne then at Aunt Catherine. If he kept this up, he might well provoke an apoplexy before Twelfth Night. None of them needed that.

"Still, poor hunting is no excuse for the number of … vegetables … served here tonight." Aunt Catherine sniffed and pushed a carrot around her plate.

"I happen to like vegetables." Darcy muttered, shoving a slightly too large chunk of cauliflower in his mouth.

"If you expect a dinner tailored to your liking, you might well consider doing your hostess the courtesy of say, letting her know of your impending visit?" Fitzwilliam lifted his glass toward Elizabeth's end of the table.

She squeezed her eyes closed and covered her eyes with her hand.

So sensitive. One would think growing up with the mother she had, she would be of a sterner constitution.

Elizabeth rang the small silver bell by her plate to signal for the second course to be brought out.

Mrs. Reynolds ushered in a team of servants who refreshed the table with a fresh tablecloth, clean china and a new array of dishes for Aunt Catherine to complain about.

"What a lovely roast chicken, and is that collared veal and rabbit curry?" Fitzwilliam tucked his napkin into his collar again, winking at Darcy, then Elizabeth.

"Mother does not prefer rabbit. She says it is gamey and tough. I have not had it in ages it seems. I happen to be very fond of it." Anne looked at Darcy expectantly.

Without meeting her gaze, he served her a large portion of rabbit curry, with extra sauce.

She took a less than dainty bite, ignoring the orangey-yellow sauce that dripped down her chin. "You see, Mother, it is quite delicious."

Aunt Catherine harrumphed and retaliated by taking a minute ladylike nibble of veal.

Oh, this was too good! If only his parents were here to witness this. No one would have expected Anne to play such a nettlesome rattlepate, but it served Aunt Catherine quite right for all the years she had tormented the rest of the family.

"I do not recall ever having curried rabbit. Is this a receipt you brought with you from Longbourn?" Anne dabbed her chin with her napkin.

Aunt Catherine groaned softly.

"No, my mother was not fond of the spices. I found it in one of the household books Mrs. Reynolds keeps." Elizabeth tried to smile.

"So you are saying you decided to serve an untried recipe upon your guests?" Aunt Catherine muttered into her napkin.

"We were not having guests when she planned it," Darcy whispered to his plate.

Anne glanced at Darcy and burst out laughing. "You must not take her so seriously, you will only encourage her."

"That is enough out of you, Anne!" Aunt Catherine slapped the table hard enough to rattle nearby china.

Georgiana sprang to her feet. "Perhaps ... I think ... Elizabeth, do you think we might all go to the drawing room now?" Poor girl was pale as the tablecloth.

"I think that a very good idea." Elizabeth rose, all grace and dignity. "You will join us, gentlemen?"

Her tone made it clear it was not a question. Fitzwilliam snickered.

Elizabeth led them out of the small dining room, down a long dim corridor of forgotten Darcy ancestor portraits, most of them as taciturn as Darcy seemed right now.

Fitzwilliam hung back with Darcy and elbowed him in the shoulder. "Pay less attention to her. You will feel far better for it."

"I did not invite her into my home to criticize everything she sees."

"You did not invite her into your home at all."

"Must you remind me?"

Fitzwilliam clapped his back hard. "Perhaps we might all relax with a game of cards."

"I hate cards." Darcy straightened his coat and strode into the small drawing room.

Aunt Darcy had not allowed him or Darcy into this room until they started university. It was not a room for high spirits, she said, but for refined company and polite behavior. Given that criteria, Anne should probably not be welcome there even now.

A dainty flip-top card table was already set up near one corner, surrounded by chairs and candles. Nearby, a small pianoforte was also well-lit and stocked with music. A large wingback chair had been pulled near the fireplace, flanked by a small table bearing several of Darcy's favorite books. Dear woman of his was doing her best to set him at ease. Lucky sot. If only Anne and Aunt Catherine would cooperate.

"I think some music would be in order whilst we digest that very fine meal." Fitzwilliam looked at Georgiana. "Would you—"

"Oh, I should very much like to play for you. You have never heard me play." Anne rushed to take a seat at the pianoforte.

"Play? You have only just begun to have lessons. You cannot perform, not even just for family." Aunt Catherine sounded just like a scolding hen. With her sharp nose, she looked a little like one as well.

"Indeed?" Anne tossed her head as her fingers danced along the keyboard.

Fitzwilliam bit his lip while Elizabeth squinted and cringed.

But there was no need. The sound that came forth was ... astonishing. Simply astonishing. She was every bit as accomplished as husband-hunter Caroline Bingley. Not up to Georgiana's standards, but few women were. Who would have thought the first time Anne sat at an instrument she could produce that?

But he and she both knew it was not the first time she had played, far from it. Why was she trying so diligently to shock her mother right now? Anne was too intelligent and too deliberate to be acting randomly.

Aunt Catherine half-sank, half-fell onto the sofa; Elizabeth caught her elbow on the way down, assuring her a graceful landing as befit her status. Georgiana perched beside her, utterly agog. No one spoke, or hardly breathed until Anne finished, then applause broke out.

"But ... but you cannot play ... only a few months of lessons ..." Lady Catherine stammered.

Anne looked over her shoulder. "What can I say, Mother, but that I am a quick study. Did not my headmistress at school declare me the best pupil she has ever had?"

"You play like one who has practiced a very great deal." Georgiana's eyes narrowed.

"You would be the best suited to recognize that, would you not? Why do you not take your turn?" Anne rose and beckoned Georgiana take her place.

Georgiana sat down and shuffled the music for a moment, settling on something that seemed to please her.

Ah, what a pleasure. She was a truly accomplished

musician—even down to her ability to select exactly the right piece for the right moment. Something light and soothing—just what everyone needed.

Anne flounced back to Elizabeth and Aunt Catherine, bouncing the sofa slightly as she sat beside her mother.

"Shall I have the tea brought in?" Elizabeth asked softly.

"I would prefer brandy." Fitzwilliam nodded at Darcy, who immediately retrieved an appropriate decanter from the locked cabinet.

"I should like that and some biscuits too, if you have them." Anne leaned back and crossed her ankles. "Playing leaves me entirely spent."

"Good thing you do not dance then, that would leave you—" Fitzwilliam muttered.

"Dance? What an excellent idea!" Anne sprang up again, grabbed Elizabeth's hand and dragged her toward Fitzwilliam. "You too, Darcy, you must dance with us. Georgiana, play us something light and merry!"

Darcy appeared too astonished to do anything but obey. Anne pulled them into a little foursome and danced—rather cheerily all told—to the tune Georgiana provided, leaving Elizabeth utterly winded. Who knew Anne could be so light on her feet, such a gay partner, and with so much endurance?

"I demand to know where you learned this?" Aunt Catherine stormed toward them.

"Is this not why you sent me to school? To finish my accomplishments?" Anne turned her back on her mother and returned to the sofa with Georgiana.

Mrs. Reynolds trundled in with a tea tray and seemed to rush back out as quickly as she could. This was not the first time Mrs. Reynolds had served during one of Aunt Catherine's visits.

Elizabeth busied herself preparing tea.

"Oh gracious! What a goose I am! I forgot entirely!" Anne pressed her palms to her cheeks, mouth open in a round 'o.'

"What might that be?" Darcy asked slowly, deliberately, shoulders tense like a man anticipating disaster.

"Miss Gifford, Miss Sarah Gifford. My very dear friend at school." Anne turned her shoulder to Darcy and faced her mother. "Did I tell you, I invited her to come and spend Christmastide with us? Her family is touring the continent right now and it did not seem right to allow her to spend the holiday season alone with only her companion for company."

"You never mentioned this to me." Aunt Catherine's entire face pursed into a deep frown, and her color shifted to something rather puce.

"Did I not? How addle-pated of me. I cannot believe I forgot." Anne pressed her fingers to her lips, a little smile peeking out from behind them.

"Do you mean to tell me, there is a guest due to arrive at Rosings Park, and we will not be there to receive her?" Aunt Catherine's nostrils flared, rather like an angry bull.

"It does look that way, but wait, what is the date?"

"The sixth of December."

"Oh, perhaps then, there is time. As I recall, her family's seat is on the far west side of Derbyshire. They might not have left yet."

"Those Giffords?" Fitzwilliam shared a wide-eyed glance with Darcy. They were a large, old, landed, and very wealthy family.

"You know of them?" Anne bounced on the sofa. "Then perhaps you will help me persuade Darcy."

"Persuade me of what?" Darcy leaned his elbow on the chair's arm and braced his chin in his hand.

"Well, I cannot rescind my invitation, that would be awful, and she would be so disappointed. Pray, allow me to invite her to come to Pemberley for Christmastide with all of us. We will be such a merry party."

Darcy's jaw dropped; he looked at Elizabeth and Georgiana. Elizabeth stammered something unintelligible.

"I ... I think ... perhaps it might be a good idea for Anne to have her friend here. They might be able to help you, Elizabeth, with all that must be done for the ball." Georgiana wrung her hands in her lap.

"A ball? You had not told me." Anne grabbed Georgiana's hands.

"We are having a fancy dress ball on Twelfth Night for Georgiana's coming out." Darcy's voice carried a low warning note.

Anne blinked several times. Perhaps she heard it for what it was. "How utterly delightful. I am so excited to be able to be here for your very special day. Miss Gifford and I can be so very helpful to you, Elizabeth. I promise—I will do everything in my power to ensure that Georgiana's ball is perfect for her in every way, and I know Miss Gifford will feel the same." Something in her voice changed very subtly; a note of sincerity perhaps?

"Do you need more help? I thought you said you felt it all was in order already." Darcy looked at Elizabeth, shrugging. She twitched her head, eyes wide and weary.

"I suppose if you are quite comfortable with the idea of another young lady joining our house party—" Elizabeth shrugged.

Anne clapped softly. "Thank you, my dearest cousin! I promise my friend will be no trouble to you at all."

"And why has no one asked my opinion on the matter?" Lady Catherine folded her arms over her chest.

Elizabeth rose. "It seems the matter is quite settled. I shall go and inform Mrs. Reynolds to expect more guests." She hurried from the room, too wise to ignore a convenient excuse for escape.

Anne cradled her teacup in her hands and leaned back. "I must tell you all about Miss Gifford."

Anne rattled on about her friend for nearly an hour. In that time, her audience dwindled until only she and Fitzwilliam remained.

"Well, that was a hand well-played." He topped off his brandy and added a little to Anne's tea cup. She liked her 'French cream,' despite her mother's disapproval.

"Whatever do you mean?" She stirred her doctored tea and took a sip, smiling.

"I am astonished you have actually done it."

"We talked about it long enough, did we not?"

He leaned forward, elbows on his knees. "But it was always a joke, never something meant to be done seriously."

"What choice have I? She has decided to marry me off to … to whoever pleases her. I can be certain anyone who would please her would never please me."

"While I cannot disagree, you could have at least warned me of your plan."

"Could I? What would you have done?" She cradled her teacup in her hands and stared into it.

"Have I not always helped you?"

"There was no time, honestly. It seems I was at home less than a fortnight before Mother stormed into the morning room declaring 'No de Bourgh is ever going to have Rosings Park. We are leaving this instant!' And so we were off to Pemberley without time to let you or anyone else know."

For anyone else, it sounded far-fetched, but for Aunt Catherine, it was entirely possible. "She mentioned something about the de Bourghs to Darcy and I. Do you know of her prejudice against your father's people?"

Anne leaned back and stared at the ceiling, sighing with the weight of the world. "You know how Mother holds a grudge. Once offended she cannot let it go—"

"Unless she sees you can be of use to her, like Darcy is to her now, then apparently she can."

"But under normal circumstances, she cannot. As I understand, when my parents' marriage articles were written, there was some contention between the families as to what was to be settled upon the couple. The Matlock side was far more generous than the de Bourghs were and Mother took it as a personal offense and statement about her worth and value. All my life she has called them 'the cheap de Bourgh skinflints' who do not appreciate the true value of anything. We have always been estranged from them."

"You are concerned she is in a hurry to marry you off to protect Rosings from the de Bourghs?" Fitzwilliam scraped his palm along his stubbled cheek.

"She does not tend to be patient with such things. I found a list on her desk of potential young men, some crossed out with notes of their flaws—flaws like an independent disposition. What am I to do?" She pitched forward and caught her face in her hands.

He sat beside her and laid an arm over her shoulder.

"You have always been my friend, Fitzwilliam, pray help me now."

"What do you want from me?"

"I am not sure yet, just be here for me when I need you." She leaned her head on his shoulder.

Poor girl sounded so very small and lost. "You know I will. I always have."

THE NEXT MORNING Elizabeth found Darcy hunched over a cup of coffee and his newspaper in the cheerful blue morning room. He sat in an unusual place—his back to the windows, facing the doorway, as though hoping to avoid being surprised by anyone entering the room. Who knew Lady Catherine—or was it Anne— had such power to disturb his equanimity even in his own home?

He looked up, a relieved smile lifting his lips, and rose to pull out a chair beside him. "Would you join me?"

"It is rather pleasing to have the room to ourselves, is it not?" She sat beside him.

He folded his paper and set it aside. "I do hope that Anne has not suddenly become an early riser amongst all her other transformations."

"As late as she rattled on last night, I can hardly imagine she will be up much before noon. This is such an odd turn of events. I hardly know what to make of it."

"I do not understand how Anne has become such a creature! As entirely un-Anne-like as anyone might imagine." He picked up his coffee cup and cradled it between his hands.

"She seemed quite proud of the transformation when she was telling me about her time in Bath yesterday." Elizabeth tried to sound nonchalant as she reached for her sewing basket. It felt unnatural to sit in this room without a piece of sewing in her hands, and there was so much to be sewn, especially in this season.

"It seems there was far more going on with Anne than any of us thought. You look troubled, what is bothering you?"

She rubbed her knuckle along her lower lip. "I do not know how much stock to put into Anne's promises. Yesterday evening, she vowed that she would do everything to make Georgiana's ball perfect. I would very much like to believe her, but ..."

He returned his cup to its saucer with a soft clink. "I cannot believe her so mean-spirited—at least not toward Georgiana—that she would intentionally do anything to ruin the event."

"Oh, my love." She touched his face gently, and he smiled. "How little you know about young ladies."

"Perhaps you should inform me."

"A girl's come out should be special and just about her. It is her night to be the center of attention and not share it with anyone else. After last night, I fear Anne will try to upstage your sister, knowingly or not—"

"You did not have a proper come out, did you?"

Elizabeth sighed and ducked her face away. This was not a subject anyone had ever broached with her before.

"That makes this ball very important to you—"

"Are you speaking of the Twelfth Night ball?" Lady Catherine swept in, skirts swishing, overdressed for the morning. She deposited herself at the opposite side of the table where she might preside over the conversation. "Of course it is very important. I suppose making the event Georgiana's come out makes a certain amount of sense, but I think it would be better—"

"The invitations have been sent. There is no changing it now." Darcy's words were low and slow—a tone that should have been a warning.

"Well I wish you had consulted with me before making such a very important decision for dear Georgiana." Apparently Lady Catherine did not heed warnings.

"Aunt Matlock thought it a very good idea." Darcy leaned forward on his elbows.

Lady Catherine sneered. "So you consulted her, did you?"

"Not precisely, Lady Catherine. She was trying to decide whether to hold a ball on Twelfth Night and asked our plans," Elizabeth forced her voice into something soft and sweet. The effort burned her throat.

Lady Catherine's brows rose, and she pounced like a bird of prey. "Then there is no question! You must allow me to review your plans, menus, decorations for the ball. Your guest will have high expectations, and you must not disappoint them."

Elizabeth gritted her teeth. "I appreciate your kind

offer, but Lady Anne left very detailed notes in her household books. We are adhering very closely to a plan for a fancy dress ball—"

"But how long ago was that? I insist you permit me to— assist you with this ball."

At least she did not actually say 'take over' even though that was clearly what she was thinking.

"You are talking about the ball?" Anne appeared at the door, Georgiana peeking over her shoulder. "Oh, what a delightful subject for breakfast!"

How was it they were up already?

Anne sat beside Elizabeth—the farthest seat from her mother— and Georgiana beside her. Mrs. Reynolds and a maid slipped in and set up breakfast on the sideboard. The room filled with scents of hot breads, cold meats and chocolate.

"Anne and I were talking about her fancy dress for the that night." Georgiana glanced at Elizabeth as though for approval.

"It is a shame you have already sent out the invitations." Lady Catherine murmured, back turned, as she poured herself a cup of chocolate. "Fancy dress can be so undignified for such an important occasion."

"Fancy dress is a great deal of fun." Anne pursed her lips in a pretty, practiced pout.

"Which is appropriate for Twelfth Night I suppose, but not for a coming out." Lady Catherine glowered at Anne.

For a brief moment it looked as though Anne might stick her tongue out at her mother. Thankfully she withheld the impulse, but her face colored with the effort.

"Anne has no fancy dress for the ball." Georgiana glanced from Darcy to Elizabeth. "We were wondering ... that is we hoped ... that we might go into town this morning and visit the haberdasher and the linen draper—"

"Please, may we cousin?" Anne clasped her hands before her chest. "We already have some very good ideas. It would be such fun to work them out with Georgiana."

Lady Catherine sat up very straight and knocked on the table with her knuckles. "What are you talking about? Certainly not. What could you know about a proper fancy dress? You will make a fool of yourself. I will manage it for you."

Anne turned her shoulder on her mother, rather pointedly. Had that been in public, it would have been considered a cut. "Perhaps Elizabeth will help us? I am certain she can determine what is good and proper for me to wear. Pray, Elizabeth, will you come to town with us and help?"

"She has a prior commitment here. We are to review the plans for the ball." Lady Catherine leaned forward, struggling to catch Anne's gaze.

"But why? Elizabeth has everything in order." Georgiana balled the edge of the tablecloth in her hands.

"Do not contradict me!" Lady Catherine all but snarled.

Enough was enough. "Of course, I think it would be lovely to spend some time with both of you. Pray excuse me while I call for the carriage and dress for going out." Elizabeth slipped out, with a quick backward glance at Darcy.

His left eye twitched just the barest bit. He approved, which was a very good thing indeed, considering that even if he did not, she would probably still take the opportunity to escape that aggravating, overbearing woman.

Lady Catherine's demands were not wholly unexpected, she was after all the same person she had been in Kent, obligated to manage everything within her reach. But now that a mistress was in place, and Pemberley was no longer in her reach, she needed to be taught her proper place, gently but firmly and undeniably.

An hour later, Elizabeth met Georgiana and Anne in the vestibule. They were laughing and chattering—no Anne was chattering, Georgiana was listening—much like Lydia and Kitty about to go into Meryton. It was good to see Georgiana seem so happy—not vaguely miserable the way she looked when Lady Catherine entered a room. Perhaps Anne was better company for her than Elizabeth had expected.

The trip into town was short, very short. As Miss Bennet, she would have happily walked the distance and much farther, but it was unseemly for Mrs. Darcy. It was one of the things she truly missed from her days as a simple Miss Bennet.

The carriage let them off at the top of the street, near the linen drapers.

"So then, you said you already had a notion of how you would like to dress for the ball?" Elizabeth held her breath. What were the chances that Anne was planning to dress as an opera dancer or a courtesan?

"Oh, yes!" Georgiana bobbed on her toes, clapping softly. "It is such a good idea. I know you will heartily approve. Anne wishes to be a phoenix."

"What an interesting choice." And perhaps a very

auspicious one. "How do you intend to create it?"

"Mother insisted I bring my red silk ball gown—just in case there would be an opportunity to wear it. I think that is why she is opposed to fancy dress. She is very fond of that gown. Still though, I can wear it. I thought if I could find black silk to sew in puffs around the bottom to look like coals," Anne mimicked the effect with her hands, "then the red dress above, a cape of yellow stuff—"

"And a red bird's mask with lovely red feathers and sparkly bits of some sort. Perhaps you might wear the feathers in your hair rather than on the mask, though." Georgiana chewed her knuckle as she often did while thinking. "What do you think? Is it a good idea?"

While it might have been fun to keep them in suspense, Elizabeth could not help but smile. "Yes, I like it very much. What is more, I think it is quite doable, and unique. I remember one of the local shops had masks—I do not recall if there were any bird masks, but even a plain one would give us a good start in creating what you have described."

"So you approve?" Anne grabbed Georgiana's hands. Something about the look in her eyes brought tears to Elizabeth's own.

What was it? Could it be so simple as the joy of finding unqualified approval? Living with Lady Catherine—it might very well be.

"I do indeed. Come, I think I saw a fabric that would be perfect for the cape you described." She linked arms with Anne and Georgiana as she had with her sisters back at Longbourn, and they paraded to the linen drapers.

The only black fabric they could find was a dull

crepe—usually for mourning wear—but it gathered nicely into puffs that would create the charred coal effect Anne desired. Better still, the yellow fabric was there as Elizabeth remembered. A soft yellow wool velvet, that with a little careful planning could have a new collar and a bit of trim attached to make it wearable as an everyday wrap as well.

Anne laughed, remarking that such economies were not heard of at Rosings and then proceeded to acquire the additional collar and trim materials Elizabeth suggested. Contrary girl!

The linen draper directed them to the milliner for a mask and feathers. Though there was none that was exactly right, they did find one that would do, in gold, not red, but a multitude of red feathers would remedy the problem.

"I cannot believe we are already done! I never have such good fortune shopping!" Anne laughed. "Usually I have to visit so many places, and I still never find what I want."

More likely, she liked to vex her mother by visiting as many shops as possible.

"It is very early to go home." Georgiana said softly, her thoughts too obvious.

"I wholeheartedly agree. I think a trip to the confectioner—no, the tea house as I am desperately hungry—is in order. What do you say?" Elizabeth winked.

"Mother does not like tea houses, but I think them charming. I would love to go." Anne giggled.

"Why does she not like them?" Georgiana seemed genuinely puzzled.

Anne lifted her nose and pulled her shoulders back in an excellent imitation of her mother. "They place one in the way of potentially low company, and that is simply not to be borne."

"In that case, I regret to tell you, she will approve of this one, there is a private room that we always have the use of." Elizabeth folded her hands primly before her.

"Oh, I think I am disappointed." Anne's shoulders slumped.

"Do not say such things or people will think you disagreeable." Georgiana glanced at Elizabeth for support.

"But I am contrary and disagreeable, entirely and completely, at least according to my mother."

They arrived at the tea house and were shown to a private nook just large enough for table and chairs with a window overlooking a flowering garden filled with stock gillyflowers in whites, pinks and lavenders. Within the cozy alcove, they seemed alone in a little world of white and frills and lace. A little shelf ran along the walls, just below the ceiling bearing odd bits of china alternating with silk flowers and ribbons. Framed pencil drawings of gardens and flowers—most of them schoolroom efforts—dotted the walls and gauzy white curtains framed the windows. A serving girl took their order and drew a curtain over the doorway.

Georgiana pulled the curtain open just enough to peek through. "Oh, it is them. My friend Miss Roberts is there with her mother. May I go and speak to her for a moment?"

"Of course, but leave the curtain pulled aside, so that any who might think otherwise will know that you are properly chaperoned," Elizabeth said.

"Thank you!" Georgiana hurried off to her friend

and waved when she arrived at their table.

"It is nice that Georgiana has friends her age and situation." Was that a touch of envy in Anne's eyes?

"Yes it is. They are sweet girls. I am very pleased that they do not seem jealous or competitive with each other."

"That is very fortunate. I hope for her that it continues. Things can change once girls are out and the marriage mart looms ahead of them."

Perhaps more had happened at school than Anne had confided to her.

Elizabeth chewed her lip. "This come out is very important to her. It has taken a long time to get her to agree it was time to come out. It is essential for all of us that her come out goes very well."

Anne looked directly into her eyes. "That is your way of tactfully suggesting that you do not want me to ruin it."

Elizabeth's cheeks colored. "You have had yours. It is only fair that she should have hers."

"I suppose you are partially correct." Anne turned toward the window.

"I do not think I understand."

"Yes, she should have her day. I agree with you. That does not mean I have had mine."

The words hung heavy in the warm alcove.

Gracious! This was more complicated that she had realized.

"I do not begrudge you your marriage to Darcy, but it is probably appropriate that you understand it has cost me a great deal. While he might not have taken the arrangement between our mothers seriously, my mother and I did. So, I never actually came out. It was not necessary as my husband was already chosen, and I did not need to meet anyone—heavens it might have complicated things, and that was not to have been borne!" She pressed her hands to her chest in another imitation of her mother. "But all that changed when Darcy threw off the plans and married you. So here I am now, nearly eight and twenty, old enough to be on the shelf, not coming out, and I must seek a match. Mother is treating it as though I have been out all along, and I can hardly disagree. I would be a laughing stock to try to come out now."

Elizabeth pressed her fingers to her lips. "I had no idea. I am sorry."

"A lesser woman might hold it against you, but I do not. I must make the best of what I have before me, and I assure you, ruining Georgiana's night is hardly in my own interest. If not for familial affection for her, you can be certain I would do nothing to taint my own chances of being seen as accomplished and agreeable."

That was actually one of the few utterly convincing arguments she could have made to earn Elizabeth's trust. "For what it is worth, I do understand a little of what you are feeling."

Anne sniffed. "I find that difficult to believe."

"My sisters and I were all out together. There was no real coming out for any of us. Nothing said, nothing done. One day we were invited to accompany my mother on her morning calls. She pinned up our hair, and that was it. She did not adhere to only one daughter being out at once, either. By the time my youngest sister was fifteen, we were all out together."

"Out with all your sisters? And without any fanfare? That is nearly as bad as never having been really out at all." Something in Anne's expression changed.

"I am sorry for you and you sisters. I had no idea we had so much in common."

"Nor did I." Perhaps there was a little more to Anne than Elizabeth had given her credit for.

Chapter 4

December 15, 1813

JUST OVER A SE'NNIGHT later, Darcy had retreated to his study after breakfast —the one bastion
of peace he could be sure of—shortly after a battle of
wills between his wife—who of herself was a force of
nature—and Aunt Catherine who did not like to be
disagreed with. All his attempts to first mediate, and
then simply to deny Aunt Catherine her demands, had
only served to make things worse. Though the encounter did not come to blows, it might have been
more cleanly resolved had it done so. As it was, the
two women merely retreated to neutral corners to lick
their wounds and plan the next encounter. That did
not bode well for anyone.

At least for now, the quiet order of the study, with everything having a place and everything in its place could soothe his ragged nerves.

Ragged nerves! Gah! He sounded like Mrs. Bennet!

A distinct knock on the study door—it must be Fitzwilliam. Darcy grunted something that resembled "come" and Fitzwilliam sauntered into the study, carefully shutting the door behind him. In one hand he cradled a brandy decanter and in the other, two crystal glasses. Was he ever far from Darcy's brandy?

"It seems a bit early in the day for that," Darcy muttered into the pile of papers on his desk. He had been staring at them for well over an hour. They made no more sense now than they had when he had started.

"If there was ever a face that needed brandy early in the day, it is the one you are wearing now. The commotion could be heard all the way from the morning room to the grand stairs." Fitzwilliam set the brandy on the desk and pulled a wingchair close— why was he forever rearranging the furniture? "Do you think your wife is still speaking to you?"

"I have not dared to find out."

"I had no idea Elizabeth had it in her to match Aunt Catherine in high dudgeon."

"Nor I—I have never seen her like that. Normally she is so—"

"Calm? Self-controlled? Reasonable?" Fitzwilliam poured two glasses and handed one to Darcy.

Darcy took a long draw. Perhaps this was a good idea. "She has never been prone to nerves or melancholy. I am completely unable to work out why she is so now. It worries me, I confess. I can only imagine that Aunt Catherine has been berating her in private as much as in my presence."

"It would be very like Aunt Catherine."

"I will put a stop to this." Darcy rested his forehead on the heel of his hand.

"How? Are you going to throw them out? You know that will not go well for you. You have spent the last year convincing my mother to see Elizabeth favorably. Throw Aunt Catherine out and it will all be for naught."

"I thought there was little love lost between your mother and our aunt."

"True enough, but Elizabeth is still the outsider. It would not take much to turn Mother's opinion against her again."

Darcy grumbled and took another large swallow of brandy, relishing the mild burn as it went down. "At least Anne has settled down tolerably. It seems that talk you had with her had a profound impact. Whatever did you say to her?"

"Anne really is a good sort. While I am as shocked as you are at this transformation, in some ways it does not surprise me."

"And how is that?"

"She and I have enjoyed a lively correspondence for well over a decade now. She always expressed herself in writing as she never could in person. She can be wickedly funny, you know." Fitzwilliam leaned back and crossed his ankles. How did he always manage to look so comfortable?

"I had no idea. You never mentioned it."

"She asked me not to. She did not think her mother would approve—Aunt Catherine probably would not have, might have insisted on reading her letters before they were posted or some other such rot. There is a widow living in one of the little cottages on the Rosings estate who would post the letters for Anne. I would address my letters to the widow, adding a special mark to let her know they were actually for Anne. We gave her a few coins for the trouble, but I think her true payment was the feeling of getting the better of the great Lady Catherine."

"I would never have expected that from Anne—it does sound like one of your schemes, though."

"And yet it was all her idea. She is quite intelligent, though she hid it well."

Darcy rubbed his fist across his chin. "I am uncomfortable with the level of deception she—perhaps both of you—have practiced."

"Yes, you are a good sort of fellow that way, and I admire you for it, to be sure. But I would warn you against issuing judgement too soon. Your own father and mother were excellent people, and you enjoyed the privilege of being the eldest son and heir, with no spares to clutter up the family."

"I know your brother has not exactly been kind on that matter." That was putting it mildly. When in his cups, or even just irritated, the viscount was quick to tear into Fitzwilliam, which was why he spent so little time at Matlock.

"It goes far beyond just him, but I am disinclined to dwell on the negative."

"I had no idea."

Fitzwilliam flicked his hand and tossed his head. "I did not want you to. I detest pity. I suppose that is something Anne and I have in common."

"You two are close?" How had Darcy missed that all this time? What other secrets did they keep from him?

"Good friends, there is a great deal we understand about one another."

A frantic pounding at the door—Darcy jumped. "Come."

Mrs. Reynolds rushed in, hands clasped tight before her. "Sir, carriages are approaching. Mrs. Darcy believes they are Miss de Bourgh's guests."

"How good of them to send word of their coming, just like—" Darcy rose, pinching the bridge of his nose, but that hardly helped against the headache that threatened. "We will receive them in the large parlor—unless Mrs. Darcy has directed otherwise."

"She suggested the same thing, sir."

"Very good." He dismissed her with a wave. It was a good sign that he and Elizabeth were thinking the same things once again. "Shall we then? I do hope these friends of Anne are more like you than the persona she has affected recently."

"So do I," Fitzwilliam murmured, following Darcy out.

Half an hour later, the family gathered in the large parlor. Though the room itself was comfortable—Georgiana even called it gay with its lively feather-print paper hangings and framed feather fans along the walls—an awkward, uneasy silence filled the room. Darcy and Fitzwilliam sat across from each other in matching wingchairs, looking from Anne to Aunt Catherine to Elizabeth. Aunt Catherine commanded the couch while Elizabeth occupied a bergère directly across and stared at Aunt Catherine as though daring her to speak. The wonder was that Aunt Catherine did not. Was it possible she was finally acknowledging Elizabeth's place as mistress?

Mrs. Reynolds announced their guests.

"Miss Sarah Gifford and her cousins: Sir Jasper Pasley, Mr. Nicholas Sadler and Mr. Gregory Wharton." Mrs. Reynolds curtsied and sidled out.

"My dear Sarah!" Anne jumped to her feet and took Miss Gifford's hands. "I am so glad you have come."

"Thank you kindly for your invitation, Mr. and Mrs. Darcy." Miss Gifford curtsied.

She was an average looking girl, pretty in the way that all girls her age were pretty, yet not memorably so. She might be a few years older than Georgiana, but quite a bit younger than Anne. That was to be expected, though—young ladies Anne's age did not generally attend school. Miss Gifford's voice was very distinct though, high and childlike. At first it sounded like an affectation, but on reflection, high and somewhat squeaky seemed like her natural tone.

"Mother, may I present my friend, Miss Gifford?" Anne forced a tight smile and glanced at Aunt Catherine who wore one of her most severe looks.

She did not reply immediately, as if she were considering refusing the connection. "I suppose."

"She is my good friend from school, and I would have you be very good to her. She deserves it." Who knew that Anne could match the severity of her mother's looks with her own?

"She does, eh?"

"Oh, Lady Catherine," Miss Gifford took a step forward and dropped in a deep courtesy. "It is a great honor to meet you. Anne has told me so very much about your great wisdom and condescension to those in your acquaintance. It is a privilege to be admitted into that hallowed circle."

Elizabeth coughed, then choked so violently Georgiana pounded on her back.

If Miss Gifford's words were less than sincere, she was an excellent actress. No twitch of an eyelid or lift of her lips betrayed any lack of earnestness.

"I see." Aunt Catherine's expression softened the way it usually did when appropriately flattered.

"And these are my cousins, Mr. Darcy, Mrs. Darcy, Colonel Fitzwilliam, and Miss Darcy."

"Pleased to make your acquaintance." Miss Gifford curtsied again.

"But who are these gentlemen you have brought with you? You did not tell me you were bringing more than your companion, Mrs. Barnes, with you." Something about Anne's expression—or perhaps it was the subtle heightening of her pitch—whatever it was felt disingenuous.

"Oh!" Miss Gifford clapped her hands to her cheeks. "What a goose I am! I must have forgotten to write and tell you. These are my cousins, they had just arrived to stay with me for Christmastide since my parents and sisters have gone to tour the continent for the season. When your invitation arrived, I hardly knew what to do. I could not abandon them, but I had already promised to see you. I was in quite a quandary. I do hope it is all right that I have brought them."

The tallest of the three, Sir Jasper according to Mrs. Reynolds, took a smart step forward and bowed. "Pray forgive our intrusion. If we are in any way inconvenient, we will find lodgings in town."

He was smartly dressed with a dark green coat and tan breeches. A pair of smudged glasses clung to his barely bulbous nose, balancing on round, red cheeks. His ginger hair—halfway between a Brutus and a 'frightened owl' style—only added to the image of an unruly boy playing at being master of the manor.

"Indeed, sir." Mr. Sadler took a large step forward, putting his shoulder slightly ahead of Sir Jasper's. What was the nature of their rivalry? "We will hold no ill-will against Pemberley if our unexpected arrival means we cannot enjoy your reputation for hospitality."

Darcy's eyes narrowed into the glare that Elizabeth often warned him not to use. But the expression did its appointed job and stopped Mr. Sadler before he drew more breath to speak. The man was thin, almost gangly, but not tall enough to be so. His belly protruded just a bit—he likely enjoyed his good meals a mite much. His short-cropped hair framed his face like a laurel wreath, in a sloppy Caesar cut—the effect was self-important and ridiculous.

Mr. Wharton cleared his throat loudly and all attention in the room turned to him. "Of course we have imposed where we have not been invited. A truly ghastly blunder on our part. If you will simply tell us of the best local inn, we shall take our leave." His booming voice matched his barrel chest and square, very square jawline that all three cousins shared. There was a certain presence about him that demanded attention. Not in an authoritative sort of way, but more a schoolboy who enjoyed being the center of attention.

Darcy probably should not judge them so severely upon their first meeting—Elizabeth warned him that not everyone made a good first impression. But the practice had usually served him well—with a few notable exceptions—for so long, it was difficult to do otherwise. Considering Anne's recent deportment, there was little reason to think he would change his mind about these men.

Elizabeth glanced at him with raised eyebrows. "It is very good of you to be so understanding—"

Anne gasped. "You do not mean to throw them out! That would be too cruel."

"Of course not." Elizabeth folded her hands tightly in her lap, her voice tight as a pianoforte string. "I only meant to say that it was good of them to understand that, with such short notice of their arrival, dinner this evening might not be precisely what they would expect, and it might take a little time this afternoon to see their quarters properly made up."

"Oh." At least Anne had the decency to blush. "I am sorry, I spoke too soon."

"Yes, you did," Darcy snapped under his breath. And that was the least of her transgressions.

"Pray, would you come help me select appropriate rooms for our guests that the maids may be set to readying them?" Elizabeth rose, so elegant, so graceful none would expect the words she was probably holding in reserve for Anne.

"Excuse me a moment as well. I would speak to the grooms regarding the additional horses." Darcy rose and followed them out.

As soon as the parlor door shut behind them, Anne began to speak. "Oh, I am so glad they are all here. Now, Sir Jasper is a baronet, so he must be accorded a room fitting for a baronet. I am certain you—"

Elizabeth drew a deep breath, but Darcy cleared his throat. "If you do not object, my dear, may I have a word with Anne first?"

Elizabeth shot her a look that would fell a lesser being. "I think that is an excellent idea. Perhaps it would be best for me to see Mrs. Reynolds alone. In fact, I think it a very good notion." She hurried away, footfalls heavy and revealing.

"Gracious, she seems a little bit tense." Anne bit her lower lip.

"That might be one word for it. Come." Darcy turned on his heel and strode to his study. Anne nearly ran to keep up.

"Close the door, and sit down." He pointed to the nearest chair and leaned on the edge of his desk.

Anne sat and looked very small. "You do not seem pleased, cousin."

"Those young men, they are not unknown to you."

"Whatever do you mean?"

"Do not take me for a fool. I will not be lied to. It is quite obvious that you know them."

Anne stared at her hands. "I admit I have been acquainted with them. They visited Sarah at school in Bath. It was a quite proper introduction."

"I suspect, nay I am certain of it, that you invited them along with Miss Gifford, without consulting Elizabeth or myself on the matter."

"Please, Darcy, do not be angry with me."

"I am angry. You have used me, and that is unconscionable! What I want to know is why." He gripped the edge of his desk.

Anne looked up to meet his gaze with a dark one of her own. "You have met my mother, have you not? Do you know what living with her is like? Can you truly appreciate what I have been through?"

He folded his arms over his chest. "I can only imagine your subterfuge and deception has not made things any better."

"Perhaps if I had been a man that might be true. I might have had another option. But I have used the only tools available to me."

"You are the owner of Rosings Park. I hardly see how you are at any disadvantage."

"You understand nothing!" She shook her balled fists. "She controls every aspect of my life. Even the staff will answer only to her. I cannot go anywhere of my own accord—the coachmen will not travel except by her orders. They will not even ready my phaeton unless she approves! All the business of the estate is handled by the steward and the solicitors. They will not deign to speak to me, either. I am a prisoner. I want to escape."

"Why have you not asked for help? Uncle Matlock, any of his sons, myself, we have always been available to help."

"If you must know," she stood and faced him, "I always expected you and I would marry and then you would manage Mother. I was simply biding my time for that to happen. It seemed the better part of wisdom not to fight when I was assured escape. But when you chose not to help me, how could I have expected anyone else to?"

"I will not accept blame for your behavior. That is upon your own shoulders."

"So you are going to dismiss them from Pemberley." She turned her back.

"I did not say that either. You have put Elizabeth and me in a most untenable position. We can hardly put them out without jeopardizing Elizabeth's reputation—but you already know that. You were counting on it."

Anne stared at her feet.

"We have little choice but to increase our house party once again. But know that you have ill-used your welcome here. You have betrayed my trust and my wife's, and that I will not tolerate. Any more behavior of this ilk and I will have you removed from Pemberley."

She turned over her shoulder and gawked. "You would not do such a thing."

"Do you truly want to test that?"

THOUGH DINNER WAS not for another hour or so yet, Fitzwilliam was dressed and on his way to the blue drawing room where Elizabeth had decided to receive their new guests before dinner. Though the room was comfortable, and near enough to the billiard room for the gentlemen to slip out for a game or two during the evening, it also signaled that they were no longer the comfortable family party they had been. A true house party was underway with all the formality that came with it.

Not the worst thing that could happen, but less than what he had hoped for when he accepted Pemberley's invitation for Christmas. Still, even with a house party, Elizabeth would never turn Pemberley into what Matlock became under his mother's rule when guests were in residence. That was something to take comfort in.

Soft strains of music drifted from the drawing room. He paused, closing his eyes to listen. Georgiana? No, the phrasing was just the tiniest bit clumsy. It must be Anne.

She sat at the piano in a tableau that resembled a painting. Flanked on either side by windows, fading sunlight framed her and the pianoforte. The blue wall behind her suited her well. It was a good color for her, perhaps better than the dusty pink she wore. That made her look a bit like a fading gillyflower, frilly and fancy, and tired. She glanced up at him, then turned her face away. Perhaps it was not so much tired as it was sad.

He strode to the pianoforte and pulled a small chair near, turning it backwards to straddle it. Balancing his forearms on the back of the chair, he studied her. "What is wrong?"

"Why should anything be wrong? I am away from Rosings. My friends have come to join me for Christmastide. What could possibly be wrong?"

"You are sulking because someone, I expect Darcy, has crossed you and threatened not to let you have your way."

"He is such a crosspatch."

"And you are a rather spoiled child."

She winced. "You call me a child?"

"When you are acting like one, I certainly will." But it seemed she already knew.

"You are just like him."

"There is no one else in the whole of England who would say such a thing." He chuckled. "There are even those who would question that we are in fact even related."

Anne plinked a discordant chord.

"He did not appreciate your additional guests." That was putting it mildly, considering the conversation he and Darcy had after he had dismissed Anne from his study.

"I did not invite them."

"Do not play word games."

"I only told Sarah that she could tell them where I was."

"And you suggested there was plenty of room for additional guests should they decide to travel with her—of their own accord, of course."

"Was that so wrong?" She laced her hands together and wrung them.

"You are using Darcy very ill, and you know it."

"Why are you so harsh with me?" She did not look at him, but the tears in her eyes glinted in the fading sunlight.

"Because you are better than this."

"You have told me that before."

He caught her chin with two fingers and gently turned her to look at him. A tear leaked down her cheek. Poor thing really was miserable, but someone had to speak the truth to her. "That is because it has been true for a very long time. You are above all this subterfuge and acting out against your mother. It is unseemly and vengeful."

"You do not understand—"

"We have long established that I am uniquely equipped to understand! We are not so different you and I, except that I have chosen to make something of myself despite my unfortunate fate as the 'spare' and my brother's continued good health and ill-temper."

"But you are a man—"

"I am glad you have noticed."

She slapped his arm. "You may go out and find some gainful employment for yourself. Unless I wish to be a governess or some such, I cannot. I am probably not even qualified for that. Truly can you see me with the charge of children?"

"You will be a fine mother someday."

"If I can get a husband—and I do not want one my mother has arranged, or even approves of." She dragged her sleeve across her eye leaving a dark streak on the light-colored muslin. "Everything she has approved of in my life has been uniformly horrid, and I am done with it. On my own merit—without any interference from mother—I have found three suitors! Three! Sir Jasper, Mr. Sadler and Mr. Wharton, they are all seeking my attention. And I like them. I like that they want to please me, that they are concerned with what I want, not Mother. Have you any idea how intoxicating that is?"

"I can imagine. But what do you really know of them? With Rosings to your name, you realize you are the kind of mark fortune hunters will seek."

"I am not so foolish to be unaware the danger. I know you do not actually believe that, but truly I am. That is part of the reason why I maneuvered to get them to come here."

He blinked hard. "Maneuvered to get them to Pemberley? What are you about?"

"Who can I trust to scrutinize my suitors? You and Darcy have always looked out for the best interest of Rosings—and my mother and I. I have watched you stand up to her and carry your point with her. I trust that you can and you will do the same now for me."

"What are you asking?"

"I want you, and Darcy, if you can convince him, to meet my suitors. I want to know your opinions of them."

"It sounds like a fool's errand. You have predisposed him to dislike them already. I can hardly imagine that you will listen if he or I find fatal flaws in one or all of them. Truly, the way you have been since you arrived, I fear that you might run off and elope with the one of which we least approve just to demonstrate that you can." He unwrapped himself from the chair and stepped to the window. The fiery orange rays of sunset faded into the indigo of night.

The Anne he once knew might have listened to him, but now? What had happened to his friend?

"You think that little of me?"

"I know you are capable of so much better."

"Would you accept my promise to … to trust your opinions and listen to them?" She laid her hand on his shoulder.

He turned to look her in the eye. "You would really do that?"

"If you promise me that you will not dismiss them for silly, petty reasons, or just because you are angry with me."

"I am not angry with you."

"You are not? Darcy is." She sniffled.

"Darcy is your cousin. I am your friend. I may think you are being petty and silly, but I am not angry. I want to see you happy, somehow."

"Then you will do as I have asked?"

"I will, but you must do something for me in return."

Her frown resembled her mother's far more than she would have believed.

"I want you to stop playing these childish games. You have got your mother's attention. She knows you are strong and intelligent and accomplished. We all do now. There is nothing more to be accomplished by your outlandish behavior."

"But what else am I to do? It is the only thing that has ever got Mother to stop forcing—"

He brushed another tear from her cheek. "Let me help you. Together, I know we can find another way, we always have."

She offered him a weak smile.

"Oh, there you are! Are you going to play for us?" Georgiana asked from the doorway.

"I should think you would be tired of that by now. Come sit with me and we can work on a duet."

Two and a half hours later, Fitzwilliam leaned back in the small chair he had taken into the far corner of the blue drawing room. With only one candlestick in that corner, he was able to observe the occupants with few noticing his lack of participation in the evening's entertainments. He had often done something similar in France, allowing him to spot more than one spy in their ranks, and a few sympathizers in the local populations. Observation was a highly underrated skill.

Darcy approached, carrying two teacups. "Elizabeth thought you might be feeling neglected."

Fitzwilliam took the proffered cup. "You married a very wise woman. Pull up a chair."

"It is not like you to sit out an evening."

"It has been an unusual day with many things to consider."

Darcy pulled a chair close and sat near him.

"Anne felt your rebuke very deeply, you know."

Darcy glowered in Anne's direction. "As well she should have. What she has done is reprehensible. I will not have her or anyone else believing they can simply use me to their ends."

"You need not become defensive. I am not disagreeing with you, only observing that your feelings have not been lost on Anne."

"You sound sympathetic to her."

"Watch her there, with Georgiana and Miss Gifford." Fitzwilliam pointed with his cup. "See how she giggled and blushed at Sir Jasper's compliments? How they are drawn by Mr. Sadler's fine dress?"

"What of it?"

"Do you not find it odd how a girl who is closer to your age than Georgiana's, older than your wife, who is no girl, but a woman, would act so very child-like? She has had so little proper training, so little exposure to society. Mayhap it would be reasonable to set expectations of her more in line with what you would expect of your sister. Georgiana has had her share of problems, no?"

Darcy grunted. He did not like to be reminded of that ghastly affair with Wickham. None of them did, but it did not change the reality of the situation. "Are you suggesting we should excuse her—"

"No, but perhaps she deserves the exercise of patience—at least a little—on her behalf."

Darcy clutched his temples. "Do you believe that she also needs the same protections that my sister requires?"

"It is not unreasonable to assume so. Anne described Miss Gifford's cousins as her suitors."

"I had gathered that much."

"She would like to be appropriately settled in marriage. Do you think Aunt Catherine is up to the task of identifying an suitable husband for her?"

"Hardly. But I promised Elizabeth that I would not meddle in the affairs of others unbidden ever again." Darcy steepled his hands before his face.

"I am not asking you to meddle. Only offer me your opinions when I ask for them. All the meddling can be left to me—I have been asked to do so, after all."

"I do not see how my opinion can be of any value. Few people impress me."

"Exactly what makes your opinion so valuable."

Darcy looked at the ceiling and shook his head. "You will excuse me, I fear if I spend any more time in your company—"

"Your entire character might be compromised. Go, go, I quite understand. But, do not be surprised when I demand your observations."

Darcy chuckled under his breath and meandered back toward the chair which Elizabeth had set aside for him for reading. Lucky sot, to have her excuse him so easily from interacting with strangers.

Fitzwilliam leaned back and resumed his observations. He might not be as predisposed to disapprove as Darcy, but not just any man would be good enough for Anne.

❧Chapter 5

December 18, 1813

THREE DAYS LATER, Darcy made his way to his study particularly early. Though Elizabeth managed most of the work of having guests in the house, somehow just their mere presence was rather oppressive. One would think that in a manor the size of Pemberley, he would not feel their presence everywhere—he barely saw them yesterday apart from dinner and the time afterwards in the drawing room. But still, at times, it made his skin twitch. Perhaps, if they had been properly invited and he had time to mentally prepare for them it would be different. But this was unpleasant at best.

The door peeked open and Elizabeth looked in. "May I?"

"Of course." He met her halfway.

She pressed a hot coffee cup and small plate with a pair of Chelsea buns into his hands.

"What's this?"

"An apology for being so ill-tempered recently." She looked down, hiding her face from him.

"My dear, you have hardly been that." Actually she had been—but their guests surely gave her good reason, did they not? He led them to the small sofa and set the dishes on the nearby table. They sat close on the sofa.

"You are being far kinder than I deserve. Fitzwilliam has been tiptoeing around me the last several days, and I think Georgiana has taken to hiding from me. I barely saw her at all yesterday. I fear I have been terrible to all of you." She did not look at him as she spoke—she almost never did that.

"Has something been bothering you? Too many guests perhaps? Or has Aunt Catherine been plaguing you again?"

"I honestly cannot say. Considering the size of the house, we do not have that many guests. It is not like at Longbourn where three visitors had us bursting at the seams. And truly, Anne's friends are not ill-mannered or inappropriately demanding."

"So you consider Mr. Sadler's insistence he only drink his own blend of tea not demanding?"

"It is a little unusual to be sure, but he did bring his own supply of tea. It is not as though he required I blend it for him myself."

"You are all that is good and kind."

"No." She sniffled and pulled a handkerchief out of her sleeve. "No, I am not. I am fussy and demanding and fear I might have my mother's nerves."

"Heavens! How can you possibly think such a thing? I assure you that is the farthest thing from the truth. Fitzwilliam has often remarked on your forbearance with Anne and our Aunt. He would rather be here with you than in his mother's home—and she is known as one of the finest hostesses in all of England."

"Now you are just being kind." She choked back a little sob.

And that was suddenly now the wrong thing to do? He craned his neck to look into her face. "This is so unlike you. What is bothering you?"

"I … I do not know." She covered her face with her hands and sobbed.

He pulled her into his shoulder and held her. What else was he to do? She had never done this before. Was there something he should say that would not make things even worse?

"I am sorry. I am sorry. I do not know what has come over me."

"Perhaps you have worked too hard. With Christmas dinner and the Twelfth Night ball, I know you have been very, very busy. I am sure it would do you very well to take some rest now. Why not go up to our room and lie down? I will tell Mrs. Reynolds to bring you a soothing tea and that you are not to be bothered for the rest of the day. Might that help set you back to rights?"

"I am not some frail little thing that I should need that." She dabbed her eyes with her apron.

"I know you are not. I have never thought that of you. But that does not mean you cannot occasionally be tired, my dear." He kissed the top of her head.

The door flung open and Fitzwilliam sauntered in. "Good morning, Darcy—oh, is this a bad time?"

"You might learn to knock." The words came out more sharply than he intended, but only slightly.

Elizabeth jumped and swiped her face with her handkerchief. "No, no, not at all. Pray forgive me—"

"She is a mite tired this morning. Pray excuse us a moment." He tucked her hand in the crook of his elbow.

"I will be fine," she whispered.

"I know, but I am not ready for so much cheerfulness from Fitzwilliam so early in the day. Allow me to walk you to our room."

She giggled and fell into step beside him.

Mrs. Reynolds intercepted them at the grand stairs, and he instructed her. She scurried away as they went upstairs.

"You did not need to be so severe with her. She has done nothing wrong."

"I was not severe with her, and she is well aware of that. I merely want to make sure no one disturbs you."

She pressed her head against his shoulder.

A few minutes later, he saw her tucked back into bed and dragged himself back downstairs.

Fitzwilliam waved a half-eaten Chelsea bun in greeting.

"I do not recall inviting you to partake." Darcy pulled the plate with the remaining bun away.

"Nor did you ask me to refrain. I am certain there are more in the kitchen." He jumped up and rang the bell for Mrs. Reynolds.

"Is Elizabeth well?"

"She takes on too much, especially with all these unforeseen demands on her. After all that happened last Christmastide, we had hoped for a simple, easy holiday this year. This—" Darcy gestured toward the study door, "is hardly what we were hoping for."

"Then let us take the better part of the day and relieve Elizabeth of their company. Georgiana's friend, Miss Roberts has invited Georgiana, Anne and Miss Gifford to visit this morning. I know the gentlemen are all interested in seeing the full breadth of Pemberley. So whilst the ladies are gone, we might ride out and take in the land, leaving Elizabeth free from the demands of any guests for the entire day."

"Save Aunt Catherine."

"I have already seen her lady's maid rushing out to find laudanum for her ladyship's dreadful headache. I expect she will spend the entire day indisposed. I believe that not being needed to manage Pemberley disagrees with our dear aunt."

Darcy sighed. More time spent in company? But if it would alleviate some of Elizabeth's suffering, it would be worth it. "All right. But only after I have had my bun." He scooped up the remaining bun and took a large bite.

Two hours later, both parties left Pemberley. Who would have thought it would take Mr. Sadler as long to get ready as it did Anne and Miss Gifford?

The sun was already high in sky, warming away the sharpest edge of the December chill by the time they made it out. An excellent day for riding: brisk but not cold, bright enough to see clearly, but not squint, enough wind to keep one from wanting to stand about stupidly. Darcy led the way through a lush field toward Pemberley's western border, while Fitzwilliam fell behind to talk with Mr. Wharton. Sir Jasper pulled closer to Darcy. Mr. Sadler seemed have his own agenda, almost as though he were riding with them only to have an audience for his horse's fancy gaits. They were showy, but utterly useless and perhaps even unwise in open fields.

"Sadler just got that horse, you know." Sir Jasper shaded his eyes with one hand and watched. "Imported from Spain perhaps? I don't quite remember all the details, but it was from the continent."

Darcy grunted. The grey speckled gelding had especially fine lines.

"Cost him a pretty penny, too. Would not even tell me how much. Afraid I will not approve I, suppose. He has quite the weakness for horseflesh."

"Indeed? I admit I appreciate a good animal." Darcy stroked his horse's neck.

"Have you a matched set of four?"

"No, though I have a very fine matched pair. One of my mares foaled twins a few years back and they grew into almost a perfectly matched pair."

"Sadler would love to see them. He dreams of having a matched foursome, but has not found one yet, poor sot. But then again, it is good for a man to have a goal and a dream. He would like his estate to be known for its horses, but it will be some time before he can achieve it."

"Any venture of that sort takes time. Patience proves a virtue in these cases."

Sir Jasper chuckled under his breath. "Not one of my cousin's finer qualities, I am afraid. Between you and me, he has been a bit spoilt from birth and would rather enjoy his pleasures now than wait for something greater tomorrow."

"You do not seem to think very well of him." Criticizing a man behind his back was not an admirable trait.

"I would hardly say that. He has some very fine qualities. I just think it best to see both a man's strengths and his flaws together. Helps one to have realistic expectations, I would say."

"Tell me of your seat, I understand it is in northwest Derbyshire."

"Lower Ilthorpe—I am excessively fond of it if I say so myself."

Darcy's brow drew up in a tight knot. That estate sounded remotely familiar, but no doubt one of his friends in the west would know of it.

"I doubt you have heard of it. The estate is not exactly well known, not yet in any case. I hope though to change that and pass my heir something greater than was passed on to me."

"You have begun improvements on your land?" Darcy gritted his teeth—not being able to remember that estate would drive him to distraction!

"Not yet, but I hope to soon. Want to make sure I am doing the right things, you know. No sense in wasting capital on efforts which will not pay for themselves. I would very much like to hear your advice. I am sure you know a great deal about improvements, and about hiring a steward. I need a competent man to assist me in the project."

"I know of several men who might be good candidates—"

Fitzwilliam pulled his horse up to join them. "It seems as though we are to have a bit of a show."

"Wharton?" Sir Jasper huffed and snorted, a little like a horse himself.

Fitzwilliam pointed into the field where Wharton was approaching Sadler at a trot. "It seems those two have been debating the complexity of those fancy gaits Sadler has been demonstrating. Wharton believes any horse can achieve those and Sadler's purchase was a foolish waste of gold."

Darcy covered his eyes and pinched his temples. Boyhood antics were not what he had anticipated when he agreed to this scheme.

"Do not be so dour, this should be amusing." Fitzwilliam sniggered behind his hand.

Somehow, what Fitzwilliam found amusing often quickly turned into disaster.

Wharton stopped his horse close to Sadler. The animals sniffed each other as the men talked. They seemed to agree on a plan. Sadler wheeled his animal around and began a trot around the perimeter of the field. Wharton followed—no great accomplishment there.

Sadler guided his horse into two low jumps over hedges between fields. Wharton managed the first, but nearly lost his seat over the second. He was going to injure his horse if he continued on in this stupid fashion!

Sadler took another lap around the field to a spot immediately across from his audience and urged his horse into a fancy high-stepping gait. Wharton followed, but when he tried to direct his horse to copy the other, the creature clearly had no idea what to do and stumbled. Wharton tumbled to the ground with a startled cry of pain.

Darcy was the first at his side, handing his reins to Sadler. "Are you hurt?"

Wharton rolled to his side, then sat. "No, no, just got the wind knocked out of me, nothing more."

"Let us help you up." Fitzwilliam took one arm while Darcy took the other, and they hauled him to his feet.

"Bloody hell and damnation!" Wharton clutched his leg. "Twisted the ruddy ankle."

Of course he did. Darcy held his breath to stifle a sigh.

"Can you bear weight on it?" Fitzwilliam asked.

"Ugh—a little, not enough—"

"If we can get you up in the saddle, I can lead your horse back. Bring the horse in close, Sadler. Darcy, help me now, steady him. Foot into the stirrup, there now—heave! Nicely done, man. Keep the horse there a moment whilst I fetch mine." Fitzwilliam returned a moment later and took the reins from Sadler. "We'll be back at the stables in a trice."

"Have Mrs. Reynolds tend him. She knows what to do. Do not bother Elizabeth." Darcy called to Fitzwilliam's back.

Fitzwilliam tossed a small salute without looking, abandoning him to Sadler and Sir Jasper's company.

"YOU DO NOT think it is broken, do you?" Fitzwilliam glanced back at Wharton.

"No, but it will not be a pretty scene when my man removes this damned boot. What a spot of rotten luck. Perhaps, though, Miss de Bourgh will take pity and read to me this afternoon to distract me from my discomfort."

Anne, read to him? That was hardly likely. She liked to be read to well enough, but detested reading aloud, unless she were allowed to have her way with it, giving unique voices to the characters and altering the story to fit her whims. Did he not know that? "How long have you been keeping company with Anne?"

"Three maybe four months, I think."

"And your cousins?"

"We were all introduced at near the same time. Sarah made the introductions, you know."

"So I have heard. But as I understand, the school mistress knew nothing of it." Fitzwilliam turned just enough to catch Wharton in a sidelong glance.

He shifted uncomfortably in his saddle. Was that his ankle or his conscience?

"I suppose that might be the case. But Sarah assured us it was all right."

"What made you seek an introduction with Anne?" Fitzwilliam grit his teeth. The answer was taking far too long.

"Sarah had told us about her very appealing friend. Who would not wish to be introduced to her? Say, what can you tell me about Miss de Bourgh?"

Clever, turning the questions around; but not very clever.

"What do you wish to know? Her favorite poets or composers? The reason she declines to wear taffeta or eat trout? Perhaps the reason she wants a Pug who she will name Mabe?"

Wharton's jaw dropped. "I was thinking something more along the lines of what confections she favored, or whether she preferred flowers from the hot house or the field."

"I am sure Miss Gifford would be able to tell you those things." Fitzwilliam certainly would not. If the man knew none of those things about Anne, he did not deserve to be told.

"Ah, very well, I see. You are correct, I should ask her. Tell me then, what do you think of Sadler's tailor?"

Sadler's tailor? Fitzwilliam had never given him a single thought. This might be a much longer ride than he had expected.

December 21, 1813

"MRS. DARCY," Mrs. Reynolds peeked into Elizabeth's dressing room. "The mumpers have begun arriving. We are entertaining them in the servants' hall as you asked."

"Very good, I shall be down to greet them in a few minutes." Elizabeth set aside the letter she had been reading. How ironic it should be from Lydia. Wickham was leaving for France soon, and they decided it best that she not even try to follow the drum. She and several other officers' wives were taking a cottage in Newcastle. What fun it would be, living with the other wives, like being back at Longbourn with her sisters.

Elizabeth pressed her eyes with thumb and forefinger. It would be a hard lesson for Lydia to learn that these other women would not pet and coddle her as she had been as the baby and favorite of the family. No point in putting that into a letter. Lydia would simply laugh at her. She wrapped her wool shawl over her shoulders and paused at the door. Charitable events were usually a pleasure to her, but seeing the mumpers had a particular poignancy. Lydia was only a few all-too-possible tragedies away from becoming one.

No, she had to stop such thinking. Darcy would never allow one of his sisters to go begging, even Lydia. Still though, war widows were far too common—how would Lydia take such a loss? Not well, no doubt. She lived in a fantasy world where she was the favorite and center of attention. Somehow, if felt like it could not last and soon life's realities would take hold and shatter her fragile perceptions.

Enough melancholy thoughts, she needed to be a cheerful and welcoming hostess for the mumpers and for her house party. With a deep breath, she headed downstairs to perform her duties.

The mumpers were uniformly gracious and grateful for the hospitality and gifts offered by Pemberley. Mrs. Darcy's wonderful qualities were highly praised. As pleasant as it was to preside over such an appreciative party, Elizabeth excused herself after a quarter of an hour. It was, after all, the proper amount of time for receiving a morning call, but more than that, there was something off in the scent of the sheep brains Cook had soaking in the kitchen. Perhaps they had gone off? Or maybe Cook was trying a new way to prepare them—either way, the effect was repulsive.

Elizabeth asked Mrs. Reynolds to deal with the matter and hurried as far from the kitchen as she could, pausing at a large vase of marigolds near the grand stairs. She pressed her face to them and breathed deeply. Not terribly fragrant, but much better than soured brains.

Soft strains of music wafted down the grand stairs. A duet? Was that Georgiana and Anne or perhaps Miss Gifford? It was a relief to know the young ladies were all getting on so well. Odd, when Anne was older than herself, to think of her as a young lady. But in many ways she was even more naïve than Georgiana.

Elizabeth peeked into the music room. With ivory paper hangings adorned with happy red poppies and yellow snapdragons, the room always felt cheerful. Sunlight streamed in through the windows that lined the longest wall, adding as much warmth as they did light. Though a mite inconvenient in the summer, this time of year it was one of the most comfortable rooms in the house. Georgiana's new pianoforte—actually three years old now, but they still called it the new one—stood in one corner, and a large harp in the other. Few knew that Georgiana played the harp. She avoided doing it in public as it drew more attention than she was comfortable with. The attention she got from her pianoforte performances taxed her nerves enough. Several sofas and chairs sat in three distinct clusters throughout the remainder of the room, with small tables nearby for refreshments or game play.

Fitzwilliam and Miss Gifford's cousins sat around the largest table, playing what appeared to be whist while the three ladies congregated around the pianoforte, ostensibly working out a piece of music. Anne's frequent, flirtatious glances toward the card table were difficult to ignore. Just inside of proper, Elizabeth bit her tongue—she really could not say anything, at least not yet. But it would still be better if Anne would stop.

Elizabeth pulled another chair up to the card table. Whist had never been her favorite game, but it was interesting—and at times informative—to watch the players. Mr. Wharton, his wrapped foot propped on a soft stool, stared in the direction of his cards, but mostly at Anne. Mr. Sadler was slightly more discreet, but not much, though he added in a few glares at Mr. Wharton, just for variety's sake it seemed. Fitzwilliam studied his hand nearly as much as he did his partner, Sir Jasper. At last he played his card.

Sir Jasper threw back his head and laughed. "I do believe that settles the game, gentlemen. I suppose you should be glad our friend the colonel has insisted that we play for just pennies."

Mr. Sadler wrinkled his nose. "It does rather seem to reduce the sport in it all."

"I am surprised to hear you say that, considering the amount you might have just lost." Fitzwilliam's brow knotted.

"Is that not the very nature of these games, losses and gains? I have found that the latter often outweigh the former. Let us increase the stakes to something interesting this hand." Mr. Sadler shuffled the cards expertly.

Fitzwilliam pushed his chair back. "Go on without me."

"You cannot stop playing after such a win." Sadler managed to look somewhat offended.

"You are still such a poor sport over that." Wharton exclaimed, folding his hands over his chest.

"I was very ill-used, very ill-used indeed by that Mr. Miller." Mr. Sadler glanced at Elizabeth. "It is possible that you may know him. I know that he had dealings in this part of the country."

"Is that so?" Fitzwilliam's eyebrows rose and he sat up a little straighter.

"Absolutely, and he is quite the trickster I tell you, for his reputation among those who have not sat with him at the gaming tables is absolutely sterling." Sadler brushed imaginary dust from his coat.

"I am intrigued." Fitzwilliam cocked a listening ear and that seemed all that was required for Mr. Sadler to pour out his tale of loss and woe, whilst his cousins exchanged aggrieved expressions, probably amplified a bit for Elizabeth's benefit.

Was it possible they did not want her to extend Mr. Sadler too much pity or favor? They were rivals for Anne's attentions, after all.

Mr. Miller's sins still remained a little unclear, at least those beyond being lucky at cards and being unwilling to play another hand after Mr. Sadler had suffered a substantial loss. And apparently, he was not the only one to wrong Sadler so.

Perhaps Darcy's dislike of the man was not illfounded.

When tales of ill-use and woe became a bit too stomach churning, Elizabeth excused herself to join the young ladies, still at the pianoforte.

"He is looking at you again." Miss Gifford giggled and leaned into Anne. "I told you he likes you, perhaps the best of them all."

Both Wharton and Sadler were staring at Anne.

Anne pressed her hands to her cheeks. "Do not say such things unless he has told you directly that it is so. I do not like being teased."

"Well, they did come all this way to visit with you. That should be proof enough of their regard." Miss Gifford winked knowingly.

"Do you have a favorite among them?" Anne asked.

"They are all my cousins. How can I possibly declare a favorite among them?"

"There is nothing wrong with having a favorite cousin, is there Georgiana?"

Georgiana started a bit and looked alarmed.

"You have to agree that Mathew, Fitzwilliam's eldest brother, is uniformly horrid."

Georgiana cringed just a mite. "I do not like him very much. What do you think of him, Elizabeth?"

All three girls turned to look at her. "I tend to find him wanting in sympathetic qualities." Jane would have been proud of such a politic answer.

Anne threw back her head and laughed heartily. Not at all ladylike, but at least it was genuine. "I shall have to remember that response. I have hardly heard anyone describe someone so disagreeable in such an agreeable fashion."

"I am not sure that made any sense." Miss Gifford tittered behind her hand.

"I have been accused of that before. Do take a turn about the room with me, Elizabeth." Anne looped her arm in Elizabeth's and pulled her along to the windows. "I do not know how to thank you and Darcy enough for allowing my guests to stay at Pemberley. We would never be permitted to have so much fun if they came to Rosings."

Elizabeth winced. That remark sounded far too much like something Lydia would say. "What exactly to you mean by fun?"

"Just the normal sorts of things young people do, you silly thing. Why just this morning, I showed Mr. Sadler the servants' passages down to the blue drawing room. It will be ever so much fun to be able to surprise people there with a sudden appearance. The servants' door is so near the curtains one may slip in behind them without anyone the wiser. He does so like to make a memorable entrance into a room."

"I was unaware of—"

"Do not be a goose, I cannot believe that. Fitzwilliam himself showed me, so I know that Darcy knows."

"Why would Fitzwilliam have shown you?"

Anne shrugged. "He wanted to talk to me the other day where we might not be overheard. I suppose he did not wish to risk Mother or a servant she has paid off hearing him ask me about—well ever so many things—he can be very nosey you know. Still, he has always been so solicitous toward me. Even before I went off to school, he would contrive ways to send me music and books I wanted, and even a few small trinkets now and then." She covered her mouth. "Oh! I was not supposed to say that—he always wanted it to remain a secret lest Mother put a stop to it. But you are trustworthy and will not tell her."

Was this really a woman of nearly eight and twenty not a girl of sixteen?

Elizabeth grasped her wrist gently. "Of course not. But you must allow me to insist that you never go into the servants' passages again."

"Now you sound like Mother! I had thought you to be eager for a spot of fun."

"I do like to have fun, but you must allow that I am far more aware of the dangers to a young woman than you are. I am sure you have heard in grand detail the plight of my youngest sister—"

Anne gasped and pressed the back her hand to her mouth. "That cad hurt Georgiana, too! Fitzwilliam told me of it in confidence. But you cannot think my friends are anything like ... him!"

"I pass no judgements on those whom I do not know. But allow me to point out two important things. Before Mr. Wickham fixed his attentions on my sister, there was a time when I was the object of his devotions. Though I pride myself—did pride myself—on my ability to understand people, I have rarely been so mistaken as with him. When he began to ignore me in favor of a local girl who had just become an heiress, then I was able to see the side of himself that he had kept hidden."

"How awful!"

"It was unpleasant. But by far the most nettlesome part of the story is that now he is my brother, and I will never be quite free of the reminder of my foolishness. So, just remember, people are often better at hiding what they are than you might be at discovering it. And second, being alone with a man, even in a place as ignoble as the servants' stairs is a recipe for being compromised. My sister was forced into a marriage that will only bring her ruin, I am sad to say, because she allowed herself to be compromised by him."

Anne rolled her eyes. She looked like Darcy when she did that. "But she ran away to London with him. That is hardly the same—"

"In some ways, that is entirely true. But should word get out into the society pages that you were discovered alone with one of your friends, you might find yourself facing ruin by compromise unless you enter into what might be an unwise marriage."

"That sounds like Mother again. Who here would possibly—"

"How many servants are there here? There are quite a number right now who do not work for Pemberley and are not under Mr. Darcy's influence. Any one of them might not hesitate to take a gossip-writer's coin. Perhaps you might take a moment today and seek out Darcy. Ask him about his dealings with the gossip-writers."

"Darcy? What would a gossip-writer want with him? He is as dull and straight-laced as—"

Elizabeth nodded slowly, very slowly, waiting.

"Oh!" Anne's face lost a little color.

"Exactly. I know you wish only to be merry and gay, but I insist that you also be wise. I must believe that those qualities are not mutually exclusive. I can see that you have been trying, very hard, and I know you can do this."

"I shall think about what you have said. A very great deal, I promise." Anne released her and picked her way back to the pianoforte.

How much were Anne's promises worth? It was very difficult to tell. Perhaps if she suggested Georgiana talk with her—but no, Georgiana would not be able to do that, it was all still too fresh for her. Perhaps Fitzwilliam might be able to get through to her.

Chapter 6

December 22, 1813

THE FOLLOWING EVENING Fitzwilliam dressed for dinner early, then slipped outside for a long walk before he would be expected in the drawing room. The clouds that haunted the sky early in the day had peeled away, revealing a sunset more pallid than spectacular. The air though was cool and crisp, with no hint of impending storms. That made it good enough.

The sun, low in the sky, cast long shadows against the bare garden stalks. They danced in the light breeze, perhaps trying to tempt him to shake off some of the heaviness he carried. Would that it could be so easy—a few gay steps amongst the crunchy deadfall and it all would slip away. Perhaps it might have when he was a boy, but no longer.

This entire affair with Anne, her suitors, and Lady

Catherine—gah! It was not at all what he had come to Pemberley for this season. Was it so wrong to want to enjoy some pleasant company? Instead, he was reminded at every turn that the marriage mart churned around him, and at some point he would be expected to plunge in himself and commit to being shut up in the parson's pound. Granted, Darcy and Elizabeth made the married state look quite tolerable, even pleasant. But, they were by far the exception, rather than the rule.

If only it were possible to be friends with a woman first, without her having any troublesome notions of courtship or betrothals. To actually be able to get to know her before the parson's mousetrap sprang, rather than after when it was too late to do anything to correct it.

How was it Darcy managed that? He chuckled under his breath. Most would not believe that making a prospective bride hate you prior to offering marriage an effective strategy, but perhaps there was something to be said for it, if the current Mrs. Darcy was an indicator.

Had he no need for fortune, he would probably have pursued Elizabeth himself, might even have won her. No point dwelling on that. Jealousy served no one and changed nothing.

Elizabeth had hinted that there was a young lady or two who was invited to Christmas dinner who might be to Fitzwilliam's taste. Those would be good introductions to have. It might even be fitting to ask Anne's opinions on their potential as she had asked him. She would probably be amused at the parallel. She always did like such things.

He paused at a barren rose bush. No doubt the

gardeners would be cutting back the canes and preparing them for winter soon. The rose bushes had been part of Pemberley's gardens for a very long time. It would be a shame to lose them.

"Fitzwilliam!" Anne ran, then slowed herself to a hurried walk toward him, dry leaves kicked up in her wake.

While Lady Catherine still remarked unfavorably on her behavior, she had done a great deal to curb its most outlandish aspects since his rebuke, proving him entirely correct. She was indeed better than she had been demonstrating.

"I am so glad to find you here." She stopped beside him and adjusted her shawl, a pretty woolen affair that was probably just barely warm enough for the late afternoon waning sunlight. Her cheeks were flushed with the exertion of hurrying—the coloring was particularly pretty on her.

"Have you become fond of afternoon walks?"

"I do not think I will ever be the sort of walker that Elizabeth is, but it is pleasant. Particularly since Mother is such a scold at dinner and in the drawing room. I find it takes some effort to prepare myself to manage her in a way that you would find acceptable."

He offered her his arm, and she took it. "I am proud of your efforts."

She beamed at him. Her smile was very pretty. "Few people have ever said that to me. It is pleasant to hear."

"It is pleasant to be able to say."

She pressed his arm a little harder. "I have seen you talking to my suitors. You have been very diligent about the favor I asked of you. Have you any thoughts on them yet?"

He huffed and pursed his lips.

"Oh, that does not sound like a good thing." The eagerness fell from her face.

"I know you have wanted me to like them all, to approve them—"

"And you do not?" She eyed him warily.

"I have reservations."

A bit of her smile returned. "Reservations; that is better than outright hating any of them, I suppose. Tell me of these reservations. I promised that I would listen, and I intend to keep my promise."

Dear girl was trying so very hard. Darcy might not acknowledge it, but she really had matured over the last year. "Mr. Wharton ..."

"You have not forgiven him for falling off his horse? I can see how that would be rather unforgivable to you." She tried to laugh, but it felt a little hollow.

"Anyone can have an accident. That is no reason to condemn him, not on its own. But, I find I cannot like the man."

"You who are all affability? Cannot like him?"

"Have you ever tried to have a conversation with him? You have not noticed he has all the intellect of a learned pig? I am surprised he does not answer most questions by grunting and pawing the ground."

She laughed so hard she clutched her belly. "Surely he is not so lacking."

"Oh, indeed he is. You should see him trying to play cards—he cannot keep a simple sequence in his mind, or even tally a few numbers without the aid of pencil and paper and even then two and three do not reliably make five. I am not joking."

"That is truly dreadful," Anne choked out from

behind her hand. "No wonder you gave up on the game so quickly the other day."

"Well Wharton was not totally to blame for that. Sadler should bear his fair part as well."

She hesitated a step. "Tell me more of him."

"Wharton is an idiot, but beyond that I detect little harm in him. But Sadler, he is more worrisome."

"I think that Elizabeth does not like him very well either."

"That alone should be reason to be concerned. She does not bestow dislike easily."

"Except on Darcy." She looked up and winked.

"Who utterly deserved it at the time, I might add, and any observer would agree. But Sadler is not that way."

"I find him very agreeable."

"Precisely what troubles me. He is very agreeable, and yet the way he speaks of others, the way he wagers at the gaming table. I do not trust him." He stopped and faced her, taking her hands in his. "I do not say this lightly. Pray listen to me. Do not entertain his attentions any longer. There is something disquieting about him in all his foppishness, something that does not add up. I cannot put my finger on it, but the instincts that kept me alive in France tell me to give him a wide berth. Pray do so."

"You make it all sound so very alarming."

"Have I not always had your interests at heart?"

"Yes," she kicked the dirt. "I suppose so."

"You just suppose?"

"You have been the best friend I could ever ask for."

"Does that not earn your trust? Will you not trust my judgement now? Pray, stay away from him." He squeezed her hands hard.

"I suppose. You have after all not taken all my suitors from me. You have not said anything against Sir Jasper—or do you have something against him too?"

"No, not for the moment at least."

"Then I may continue my friendship with him?"

"Carefully, Anne. I do not wish to see you hurt."

"I am sure you will find no reason to disapprove of him. He is a baronet, after all. That should mean something about his character."

He snorted and she looked offended. Perhaps it was a bit ungentlemanly, but if she only understood the ridiculousness of her remark! Her ignorance ... he sighed.

"How little you know of society, my dear cousin." He placed her hand in his arm and continued walking. "I would rather not be the one to teach you of it. Perhaps—and I cannot believe I am saying this—it would be good for you to read the gossip pages that Darcy so detests. I do not think he even permits them in the house—"

"My school mistress did not, and Mother does not even read the newspaper."

That was hardly surprising, and explained a great deal of Aunt Catherine's political opinions.

"I will procure them for you and have them sent to your chambers. We might discuss what you learn from them."

She giggled. "I think I will like your approach to education."

As long as Darcy did not find out, it should be a very interesting exercise. And if Darcy did discover, it would be interesting in an entirely different way.

DARCY PUSHED HIS chair back and dabbed his mouth with his napkin. It was tempting to blame Aunt Catherine's particularly bad humor over dinner on her continued headache. But that excuse only went so far, and she had long since used it for all that it was worth.

There was no venison on the table-although game birds abounded, they did not suffice. Sheep brains should be fried in a crust and served with gravy—no other way. The roast potatoes were hard and the carrots too soft. He pinched the bridge of his nose. Perhaps a bowl of gruel would have better satisfied her. Another night like tonight and he just might suggest it.

How had Elizabeth managed to keep her patience with his aunt? She was a wonder. Who could blame her for suggesting rather abruptly that they all retire to the drawing room? While he would not have minded a little male company over cigars and port, it really was too much to ask her to bear Aunt Catherine all alone.

In the drawing room, Anne and Miss Gifford nudged Georgiana who approached Elizabeth. "Might we play some parlor games tonight?"

"Those ruckus, rowdy things?" Aunt Catherine sniffed. "I have no use for them." She retreated to a large chair near the fireplace, her nose in the air. On the way she caught first Fitzwilliam's eyes, then Darcy's, and looked to the empty chairs near hers. They were being summoned to an audience.

"I think it a marvelous idea." Fitzwilliam stepped forward. "A game of Move-All is just the thing to wake us up after dinner. How many shall play?"

Elizabeth edged half a step back. "I am content to watch, thank you, but do go on and enjoy yourselves." She moved to the sofa near the table where the tea service and biscuits awaited their leisure.

"You may have my share in the amusement as well." Darcy joined her, leaving Aunt Catherine glowering at them all.

Probably just to spite them, she turned her back and continued to sit alone by the fireplace, without even a book for company. They might all pay for it later, but for now, having a little distance from her was welcome.

He sat beside Elizabeth. Tiny, tired lines creased the edges of her eyes.

"Perhaps you should retire early tonight. You look exhausted," he whispered.

"It has been rather a long afternoon. Lady Catherine decided to review all the menus until Twelfth Night. Mrs. Reynolds tried to object and sent for me—the entire production was unpleasant and unnecessary."

"I am so sorry—"

"But it was nothing compared to Lady Matlock's attempts to take over last year." The corner of her lips lifted in a tiny bit of mischief.

"If that is supposed to make me feel better, it does not."

"I should not tease you so, I know. But it always helped when dealing with Mama—"

"So of course it should be a good strategy in dealing with all difficult relatives." He chuckled softly. "If you want me to suggest they leave, I will."

"I am not prepared to deal with the consequences

of that—not just yet in any case."

"I am not sorry to hear it. But look, it seems like Georgiana is having a merry time." He pointed with his chin.

Fitzwilliam stood in the center of a circle of chairs and cried "Move all!"

Everyone leapt to their feet and scrambled for a seat, save Wharton of course who sat nearby, sulking just a mite that he was left out of the fun. Served him right though for being so stupid about his horse. Anne and Miss Gifford dove for the same seat and ended up in an ungainly laughing heap on the floor instead. Anne gave up the seat to her friend and took the center of the circle.

"Have you noticed that Anne is paying very little attention to Mr. Wharton and all but totally ignoring Mr. Sadler?" Elizabeth worried her bottom lip between her teeth.

Did she know what an alluring gesture that was?

"No, but now that you mention it, it does seem her behavior has changed."

"I cannot help but be glad for it, at least with regards to Mr. Sadler. I think little of him."

He sat up a little straighter. "Has he been paying Georgiana any attention?"

"Fitzwilliam suggested that she is not officially out and it would be in poor taste to do so. I wonder if he made a suggestion that Anne cease her interest in him? The change in her behavior seems very abrupt."

"It is possible. It seems he has great influence with her."

The group rose and scrambled again. Anne and Fitzwilliam ran into each other, stumbling and catching one another in a tangle of arms and legs.

"Have you ever considered the possibility—" She tipped her head toward the pair.

"What? Of Anne and Fitzwilliam? You promised me long ago that you would not indulge in match-making of any sort."

"You know I eschew the sport. I just wonder. Watch them together, they seem to have, well, it is hard to say. Perhaps an understanding of one another that is rather uncanny."

"You know they are apt to fight like a fox and a hound."

She patted his hand, just a little condescendingly. "While that is not something you would tolerate well in your home, there are other dispositions who do not find it nearly so disagreeable."

"He has never made mention of any attraction toward her to me."

"I wonder if he is aware of it himself."

December 23, 1813

"SIR." FITZWILLIAM'S VALET appeared in his room, a peculiarly somber expression on his face. The man was always serious and professional to be sure, but this was something different. And it did not bode well.

"Out with it, man." Fitzwilliam rose from his all-too-comfortable chair where he had been scanning the society pages to discuss with Anne later that afternoon. For better or worse, the *ton* had not disappointed, providing ample points to discuss—and laugh over—with her.

Who would have thought she could have ever

equated title with good behavior?

"Lady Catherine wishes an immediate audience."

"Did she deign to offer a reason for the request?"

"No sir, should I ask?" Something in the way his eyes creased at the corners suggested he would rather be asked to walk ten miles in a blizzard.

Who could blame him?

"Not bloody likely she would give you an answer if you did." He tossed his paper aside and straightened his coat. "Where is her ladyship?"

"In the sitting room near her chambers, sir."

He nodded at the valet and strode out. Perhaps he should not obey her orders so quickly and feed her notion that she was some sort of matriarch here. But the alternative was listening to a quarter of an hour lecture on timeliness. An even less appealing prospect.

The corridor of the family wing, lined with portraits of the recent Darcy generations, felt far more occupied than it actually was. Uncle and Aunt Darcy looked down on him, smiling tolerantly while a very young Darcy, still in a dress, stood beside them, looking as serious then as he did now. Across the hall and several yards down, Uncle Darcy's parents seemed to gaze at him. Uncle Darcy was the spit and image of his father, but Darcy resembled his grandmother—definitely a boon for him. Fitzwilliam snickered under his breath. What would the senior Darcys have thought of Lady Catherine? Given their expression, probably what Darcy did: ridiculous, but to be tolerated for the sake of family.

He peeked into the sitting room. No doubt she had arranged it to her liking, with a single, large armchair, upholstered in bright blue flowers, at the top of the room, presiding over the rest of the seats, much like she arranged her favorite parlor at Rosings. Other smaller, duller seats—small chairs and a settee covered in browns and ivories deferred to her presence, looking small and insignificant in her shadow. The walls were paneled in some dark wood—oak perhaps?—giving the feeling of a court proceeding more than a conversational space. So very fitting. No wonder she chose this room.

"Do not just stand there so stupidly, come in, and do close the door." She waved at him without standing. Her ample skirts matched the colors on the chair—did she plan that? It would not be beyond her.

He complied, very slowly.

"Enough of your dawdling, sit down, I have important matters to discuss with you." She rapped her knuckles on the wooden chair arm.

In the far corner, almost hidden by a large globe, he spied a leather wingchair. That should do nicely. He dragged it into Lady Catherine's courtroom and placed it as near as he dare to her dominant seat.

Her face crumpled, like a piece of ill-used foolscap. "Are you comfortable now, nephew?"

"Quite, thank you for your concern." He sat and crossed his legs in as casual a pose as he could muster without his banyan and nightcap.

"No more nonsense. This is absolutely serious." She brandished a letter at him, waving it wildly so he could neither read any of it or take it up himself without risking tearing it out of her hands.

"Perhaps you should tell me what is concerning you."

She smoothed the letter in her laps. "I have been making inquiries you see, and at last I have received a response from my solicitor in London."

"Is there some problem with the business of Rosings?"

"No, something far more important."

"Is your health in jeopardy?"

"Do not be ridiculous. You see I am entirely hale."

"Then what is this essential matter your solicitor writes to you about." Patience and diplomacy were qualities best left to higher ranking officers.

"Deception, Fitzwilliam, of the most foul and dangerous kind." She waved a pointing finger at him.

He pinched the bridge of his nose and bit back a thousand curt responses. "If you do not tell me in detail what you mean, there is little I can do to assist."

"Those men who came with that Gifford girl, they are not what they seem."

He sat up so abruptly his back pinched. "What do you mean?"

"One of them is a de Bourgh. That Sir Jasper as he calls himself—"

"He is not a baronet as he claims?"

"He is indeed, but he is also a de Bourgh." Aunt Catherine snarled the name like a curse.

"How is that possible? His name is Pasley, is it not?"

"It is all right here." She shoved the letter at him.

At last! There might be some sense to be made out of this! He scanned the neat, though somewhat over-ornamented script. In the middle of the page was a carefully drawn de Bourgh family pedigree. He traced it with his finger.

There was Lewis de Bourgh's line, ending, for now at least, with Anne. Following back and down several other branches of the family, things became muddled and unclear. No wonder Sir Lewis was content to leave Rosings Park to a daughter, with that much death among the male progeny, the scrambled lines and younger sons adopted into other houses as heirs. What a jumbled mess!

"See here!" Aunt Catherine jabbed at a spot in the pedigree.

Sir Jasper's grandfather, a junior de Bourgh son had been adopted by a Pasley and taken that name. Got himself made a baronet—probably an interesting story there—but there was no doubt, the Pasley baronetcy were really de Bourghs.

"There! It is exactly as I have told you! The de Bourghs are trying to retake Rosings Park, and I will not have it. I insist you put a stop to it."

"What do you expect me to do? He has done nothing objectionable save court your daughter whilst being distantly a de Bourgh." He shoved the letter back toward her.

"I never approved of him in the first place. He has no permission to even speak to her. Keep him away from her and her away from him."

"I am not her keeper, madam. Surely you can see the futility in the exercise."

Her eyes narrowed. "You take great delight in vexing me, I know. But you will do your duty. You must! The family cannot fail us again. Keep that man away from my daughter."

"Short of marrying her myself, how might that be accomplished?"

"How can you say such a thing? You marry Anne? That would be—"

"Consider your words very carefully, Aunt Catherine. It is not wise to insult the man of whom you are asking a large favor." He turned his officer's glare upon her.

She started and pulled back. Apparently she had never seen that look—but perhaps she needed to again.

"Just keep Sir Jasper from my daughter. He is not to be trusted, mark my word. That family is not to be trusted. They are devious and always seeking to get what they do not deserve and what they cannot afford."

"You were insulted by Sir Lewis's parents decades ago, but that hardly condemns the entire family."

"You would be surprised how little one branch of such a family differs from another. They are all devious and difficult. Are you going to help me?" She shook a long, pointing finger at him.

"I have detected nothing objectionable in the man. I just told Anne as much and can hardly go back on my word—"

"What right have you to be giving approval to any of those men? Why would she turn to you to ask such things and not me?"

"Do you really want an answer to that question? I would be happy to give it to you, but I do not think you will like it very much." He stood and towered over her.

She shrank back a mite.

He should not be enjoying this as much as he was. "I am sorry you have put yourself in such a position with your daughter that she is more likely to do the opposite of what you would ask than to obey you. But I will not insist she bend to your will simply because it is your will. Out of respect for you, I will however, discuss the matter with Darcy and obtain his opinion on Sir Jasper. I will plan my course of action according to that. Do not ask any more of me."

She stammered something hardly worth listening to. He turned hard on his heel and marched from the sitting room.

The nerve of her! The unmitigated gall! Trying to use him like some servant, all the while thinking no better of him than the rest of his family did. But for his friendship with Anne, he would wash his hands of Aunt Catherine and Rosings Park entirely.

He stormed down the great stairs and straight for Darcy's study, several startled maids almost tripping in their haste to get out of his way. If there were any justice at all in the world, Darcy would be alone and willing to accept his company.

The door was closed; he raised his hand to knock and paused. It would not do to pound the door like he was ready to break it down. He drew a deep breath and knocked like a civilized gentleman. More or less.

"Come."

He drew another deep breath before entering the room.

"What happened? You look like the very devil himself!" Darcy half-rose from his chair behind the massive desk.

"Good to see you too, Darce." He fell into the wingback he had left near the desk the last time he had been in the room and assumed the sloppiest posture possible; just because he could.

"Dare I ask?"

"I assume you are intelligent enough to guess. I was called into a most unwelcome audience just now."

Darcy clutched his temples. "What did she want?"

"Apparently the de Bourghs—or rather a de Bourgh—has indeed come."

Darcy raked his hair. "What did you tell her?"

"That I did not give one whit for her opinion on the matter on whether he was a de Bourgh or a Smith, and I would consult with you and make my decision based on that."

"I do not imagine she was happy with your answer?"

"I did not stay to find out."

Darcy snorted a laugh. "Nor would I. What is your opinion of Anne's suitors?"

"One is an idiot, another a fop who reminds me far too much of another attractive young man in our acquaintance."

Darcy winced, nodding. "It is a bit of a relief to know it is not just simply me seeing him at every turn."

"For what it is worth, I insisted Anne discourage any future interest on their part."

"What of Sir Jasper?"

"Do not tell me you do not like him." Fitzwilliam rolled his eyes—no he should not do that, it was a bad family habit, but truly, how could he be expected not to at such a moment.

"You do?"

"I would not go that far. But I did not find anything objectionable about him."

Darcy looked away.

"No—pray you do not dislike him for being a de Bourgh!"

"I wish that were the case. Then you could simply argue me away from it."

"Then what is it?"

Darcy drummed his fingers on his desk. "I wish I could say. But, I cannot quite put a finger on it. Elizabeth has noticed it, too. I have sent out some discreet inquiries—"

"You have a network of spies?"

Darcy did fit the picture of a spy master.

"Mutually beneficial acquaintances. In any case, I anticipate hearing back from them in the next several days, assuming they know anything of the young baronet."

"What do you suspect?" Fitzwilliam leaned his elbows on the edge of Darcy's desk.

"I would rather not say, in case my suspicions are incorrect. I would not harm his reputation in your eyes simply because I am overcautious."

"I hope you are wrong for Anne's sake. I think she may be setting her cap for him—"

"I would have her avoid that for now, if it were possible." Something in Darcy's expression made his words more command than suggestion.

"I dread telling her that, especially after I have all but given her permission— she will think me mean-spirited and capricious."

"I pray that I am wrong, but if I am not, she will thank you for it."

"Even if her mother gloats over her victory?"

"Yes, even then."

Heavens, what did Darcy suspect?

❧Chapter 7

THE NEXT DAY, Elizabeth put Georgiana in charge of the evergreen gathering party. She would have liked to have gone herself, but a little time to rest and spend with her husband was too much to relinquish, even for the fun of gathering Christmastide decorations. Who knew that having even a moderate sized house party could be so exhausting?

Darcy came to her dressing room and joined her on the small couch they had placed near the fireplace for just such a purpose. The room had been very different when she had first taken ownership of it, but they had slowly shaped it into a private sanctuary they could share, insulated from the cares of the estate. No business was allowed within, not accounts, not menus, no talk of spring planting, nor autumn harvests.

He seemed to appreciate those rules as much as she.

The walls were covered with a warm green silk, not entirely to her tastes, but tolerable enough when decorated with florals, landscapes, and the small family portraits she had pilfered from other rooms in the house. Little of the original furnishings remained; they had been heavy and fussy. But with so many rooms in the house, she soon found light and elegant pieces to take their places. Tables with smooth elegant curves, chairs with soft seats and pillows, and a marquetry writing desk near the window where all her personal correspondence was written. Several crystal bowls of dried lavender perfumed the air, just enough to be noticeable and set the room apart from the rest of the house as their special space.

Darcy slipped his arm over her shoulder and sighed. "There has not been enough time for this."

"No, there has not. I had not anticipated how much time I would be spending playing chaperone to so many young ladies." She laid her head in the hollow of his shoulder. How warm and right and restful it was.

"We seem to be making a habit of uninvited guests at Christmastide."

"I hope that twice does not make a habit. But then again ..." She winked up at him.

"Next year I shall have the door knocker taken down on the first of December."

"If I did not know you better—"

"Just wait and see. I am not joking." So somber and serious he tried to be, but his eyes twinkled just a bit.

"Well, I doubt Anne will be with us again next year, I expect she will be married 'ere long."

Darcy sat up a little straighter and peered at her, merriment lost from his expression.

"Have you not noticed how it seems she has brought all her powers of pleasing to bear upon Sir Jasper in the last few days? She was just this side of improper last night, and earlier today in the morning room—"

He dragged his hand down his face. "Pray tell me, Georgiana is not going to do this same thing—fill our home with suitors none of whom we particularly approve."

"Georgiana is hardly Anne. I do not detect that she is in any hurry to leave her paternal home. Moreover, her scare with … ah … him … seems to have made a genuine impact on her. She dearly wants your approval, so I doubt she would consider anyone you disliked."

"I fear you are right, Anne has no respect for her mother. I wish it were not so, but it is not difficult to understand. At least it seems she listened to Fitzwilliam's dislike of the other two would-be suitors."

"For that I am glad. As it is, I fear I may have to step in and curb her behavior. I think the parlor games are getting a bit too exuberant. Sir Jasper does not seem to object, though. He never leaves off an opportunity to partner with her in the drawing room." She rubbed her knuckle against her lips.

"A lady's imagination is very rapid; it jumps from admiration to love, from love to matrimony in a moment."

"You sir, are impossible. As I recall, it was you whose mind jumped rapidly from admiration to love, not mine."

He silenced her with a kiss. Several.

A little time alone was indeed a very good thing.

That afternoon, the house party busied themselves tying red ribbon bows on their evergreens and decorating the public rooms with them. Elizabeth restrained Mrs. Reynolds from correcting the over-eager decorators. Best correct—or rather improve—their efforts whilst they were not in the middle of their fun. Mrs. Reynolds did have to clear them out of the large parlor, though, to make way for the farmers who brought in the Yule log for the fireplace—nothing could disturb those efforts. How Darcy loved presiding over Pemberley's Yule log tradition.

After dinner, the house party retired to the parlor and gathered around the fireplace. Darcy anointed the log with oil, wine and salt, then he and Fitzwilliam lit the Yule log together, just as they had last year. Soon the warm, raspy smell of wood smoke laced the room.

Elizabeth enjoined everyone to hold hands in a circle. She took Darcy's hand. Interesting, Anne stood between Fitzwilliam and Sir Jasper, holding Fitzwilliam's hand quite comfortably, but barely touching fingers with Sir Jasper. Between Darcy and Georgiana, Lady Catherine barely pressed the backs of her hands to theirs.

Darcy cleared his throat. "Let us take a moment and consider the year past. Our faults, mistakes and bad choices. Let us allow the flames to consume those that we may begin the coming year with a clean slate. With that as our starting place, let us purpose to learn from what we release and improve our faults, correct our mistakes and make improved choices."

He squeezed her hand hard. They lingered a moment longer then released the circle. Lady Catherine retreated to a chair in the corner, continuing her habit of silent sulking after dinner. But since it was silent, how could anyone really object?

Mrs. Reynolds led in several maids bearing trays of cider, apples for roasting, bread and cheese for toasting. Fitzwilliam took charge of tying strings to the apples and hanging them off the nails in the fireplace to roast. He gave the bread and the cheese over to Mr. Sadler, whose figure hinted he might have some expertise in toasting them.

The warm, welcoming smells of treats prepared over the flames of the Yule Log permeated the parlor, the smells of winter and family. Darcy handed Elizabeth a mug of cider and offered her a seat near his, toward the back of the room. Away from the fire, it was a bit cooler, but it did provide a lovely vantage point to watch the young—and not quite as young people—enjoy themselves.

When had she stopped thinking of herself as a young person?

"How about a game of Hot Cockles?" Mr. Sadler called, moving a wooden chair into the center of the room?

Elizabeth drew breath to protest, but Anne cut her off. "I love a game of Hot Cockles!" She flounced to the chair and sat down. The remainder of the party formed a loose circle around her.

"Then I will take my turn at guessing first." Fitzwilliam followed her closely.

She huffed and frowned, eyes on Sir Jasper. "Very well. I do so hope you are a good guesser though."

Fitzwilliam winked at her, but she glared in return. He knelt in front of her, tied on the blindfold, and placed his head in her lap.

Miss Gifford giggled, but Georgiana looked vaguely annoyed.

Anne pointed at Miss Gifford who stomped toward the center of the room, tapped Fitzwilliam's shoulder and ran back to her place with the same heavy footfalls.

Fitzwilliam turned to face the group. "The only one with steps so heavy is Wharton."

Wharton laughed a little too hard, pointing at his still tender ankle. "T'was not me."

"I guess I must pay a forfeit and try again." Fitzwilliam returned his face to Anne's lap.

Mr. Sadler tip-toed up and tapped Fitzwilliam's shoulder, looking much like a Gillray caricature.

"Was that Miss Gifford's lightness of step?"

"Hardly," Sadler laughed. "What happened to your vaulted powers of observation?"

"He has lost them in the presence of so many lovely ladies." Sir Jasper winked at Anne. "You have had your turn, let another try." He strode up to Fitzwilliam and held his hand out for the blindfold.

Fitzwilliam handed it over, but did not appear too pleased about it. His jaw clenched as Sir Jasper placed his head in Anne's lap.

Darcy leaned into Elizabeth's ear. "Is there something we may do to stop this? He is far too close to her."

She bit her lip. "It will be easier if you would play something with us."

He sighed. "Very well."

Perhaps something a bit more sedate would suit them all. She slipped away and retrieved a large wooden platter from the cabinet where the board games were kept.

"Was it you who tapped me, Miss Darcy?" Sir Jasper asked, untying his blindfold.

"Yes, sir, it was."

"You see, that is how this game is played." He waved the blindfold at Fitzwilliam.

Elizabeth took Darcy's hand and moved toward the center of the room. "I have another game! Twirling the Trencher."

"I do not know that game." Miss Gifford moved aside for Elizabeth to take the center of the circle.

"We stand in a circle with one in the middle to spin the trencher. Like so." Elizabeth spun the plate that cast dancing shadows in the firelight. "While the plate spins you call out a name and that person must catch the plate before it stops twirling. Whoever lets the plate fall must pay a forfeit." She spun the plate again. "Darcy!"

He jumped and hurried to catch the plate and spin it again. "Georgiana!"

She ran to the center. "Fitzwilliam."

He sauntered to the middle and caught the plate just before it rattled to the floor. "Anne."

"Sir Jasper!"

He stumbled over the edge of the carpet and nearly fell trying to get to the plate, but caught it just in time. "It seems I am not nearly so nimble footed as you, Colonel Fitzwilliam." He saluted, but it seemed more mocking than friendly. "Perhaps we might take a short break to enjoy those sweet-smelling apples."

The men brought a low table into the center of the room, with cider and small plates. Fitzwilliam supervised serving, though Anne refused her portion. He beckoned her away from the rest, to a dark corner of the room, near the game cabinet.

Elizabeth edged a few steps back, closed her eyes and concentrated. Yes, they were just loud enough to hear. Eavesdropping was certainly impolite, but sometimes was absolutely necessary.

"Why are you so disagreeable tonight?" Fitzwilliam asked.

"I could ask the same of you."

"What have I done to make you think I am disagreeable?" He sounded a little like Darcy exasperated.

"You have been interfering with Sir Jasper and me all night! Tripping him as you did was a particularly low maneuver." Did Anne just stomp?

"I did no such thing. It is not my fault if he is clumsy."

"It seems you are trying to keep me apart from him tonight."

Fitzwilliam huffed, long and low. "There are some concerns."

"Concerns? What concerns? You told me—I asked you specifically, and you said it was all right." Her voice tightened, high and shrill. "You have been talking with Mother."

"What do you mean? You know—"

"You are not as clever as you think. He has already told me. He thinks she might hold his pedigree against him, but it is all stuff and nonsense. I would have thought you better able to see through her blather."

"This is not about that."

"So it matters not to you that he is a de Bourgh?" She sniffed and her skirts swished. She was probably turning her back on him.

"I could not care less what his name is. You ought to know better than to expect me to side with her on something so petty."

"Do I? It seems awfully convenient that you have suddenly started agreeing with Mother that none of my suitors is suitable."

"While I grant it has never happened before, chance alone dictates that we will agree at one time or another. And, if you would have bothered to listen, you would realize that I have said nothing against Sir Jasper, only recommended caution at this point. Darcy is uncertain—"

She whirled, most likely facing him with her mother's angry glare. "Darcy? Now you use Darcy against me? How could you? It is his fault I am in this situation in the first place. How could you take his side?"

"I have taken no side but yours."

"Really? I can hardly see how you have taken my side. I thought you were my friend. I trusted you. But now I can see I have been keenly mistaken. You care nothing for me at all."

"Be fair, Anne. Just because I am not anxious to let you have your way does not mean I am against you." Fitzwilliam's voice shifted just a bit, as though he were really touched by her accusations.

"It means so for everyone else. Why should it be different with you? Truly, I do not want to see you right now, and I may never speak to you again." Anne stomped and dashed from the room.

Elizabeth opened her eyes, trying not to stare.

Fitzwilliam watched her go, fists balled and teeth clenched. He was angry, no doubt, but his eyes—they suggested something more than just that. Darcy wore that expression when he was deeply hurt.

Did Anne have any idea she had just wounded her greatest ally? Would she even care if she did?

December 25, 1813

CHRISTMAS Day began with holy services, as was their custom, but Darcy led them home soon after. Mrs. Reynolds was an excellent woman, but still, Elizabeth insisted that she needed to oversee the remaining preparations herself. After Christmas plans had to be cancelled last year, nothing must go wrong this year.

Despite all efforts, nothing Darcy said could convince her otherwise. But really, she was no more fretful than his mother had been over such events, so he bit his tongue and left her to see the remaining few details in order. Still though, was it normal for a woman to be so concerned over such things? Fitzwilliam would have him convinced he was inventing things to worry over, but he was not so certain.

Later that evening, music greeted them at the doorway of the drawing room. Georgiana and Anne were playing a duet. Extra candles and mirrors filled the room with gaiety and light; the smells of the fresh evergreen boughs might have something to do with that as well. He relinquished Elizabeth to her duties as hostess and retired to his favorite chair until he would be pressed into a similar service.

How different this was to other Christmas dinners. The one Caroline Bingley had hosted had probably been no less well planned, but everything about it was prickly and uncomfortable, like a coat that did not fit across the shoulders. Pull and tug and adjust as one might, nothing made it feel comfortable. That evening could not have ended soon enough.

Though perhaps, not his first choice in activities, tonight was no major burden on him, and he even anticipated some pleasure in it. Why was tonight so very different from the other?

Surely, Elizabeth had something to do with it. Her presence and social acumen gave him peace amidst so many people in his domain. That was another difference. Pemberley was his domain. To be in his own territory and know he was safe from the gossip-writers and others who would seek to intrude upon his privacy; that made a substantial impact, too.

His guests here were known to him, and if not friends, at least on friendly, neighborly terms. On the whole, they looked out for one another's interests. Not like the crowds in London who barely knew with whom their elbows rubbed. Yes, that was another material difference.

Perhaps he had dreaded entertaining at Pemberley more than he should have. Elizabeth would enjoy hearing that.

Fitzwilliam sauntered in and sat near Darcy. "It is a pleasure to hear the two of them play together. They do it very well, I think."

"Considering it was not until just a few weeks ago that anyone even knew she played, I would say it is utterly remarkable. I would not have thought her and Georgiana to be able to get along so well, either. My first concern was that they would have nothing to say to each other, both being so quiet, and then that Anne would utterly overpower her when I discovered she was not what we thought."

"What you thought, Darce, I have known better

for quite some time. Now that she has come under better regulation, I find it a pleasure to see her living for once, not cowering in her mother's shadow."

"You think the time here has done her good?"

"Very much so. Your ladies here have been very kind to her, something Anne has not known a great deal of. I do not know this, for Anne has not actually said, but I heard Georgiana suggest that perhaps, just amongst themselves—Georgiana, Elizabeth and Anne—they might treat this night as Anne's come out, so she would have a night she could mark in her own mind as hers."

"Elizabeth has agreed to this?" Darcy ran his knuckles along the edge of his jaw.

"I am not sure there was anything actually official to agree to. But yes, I believe that Elizabeth found the idea pleasing. Knowing her, she probably instigated the notion and allowed Georgiana to consider it hers. I recall her saying all young ladies should have a special come out."

"She never breathed a word of it to me."

Fitzwilliam shrugged and avoided eye contact.

"What I wonder, is how it is you manage to be privy to such conversations? One might suppose—"

"Look, Elizabeth approaches! And with some very appealing company." Fitzwilliam rose. Though he turned his face aside, there was a decidedly guilty look in his eyes.

Two young ladies followed Elizabeth; the daughter of a local knight, Miss Susannah Camelford, and the daughter of a major silk mill owner, Miss Lora Audeley. Both were attractive girls in their second—or was it third season out? Neither was considered near to being on the shelf, but it was notable that they were yet unmarried. Their dowries were just sufficient to catch a titled man, and their mothers had high aspirations for them both. How much matchmaking was afoot here?

"Fitzwilliam." Elizabeth extended her hands toward him. "May I introduce you to some of our friends?"

He took a long, appreciative look at Elizabeth's charges. "I would be very happy to make their acquaintance."

The girls giggled—was that a requirement of being a young lady in these times—to giggle at the attention of a single gentleman?

"May I present Miss Camelford of Langhey Green and Miss Audeley." The girls curtsied in the accepted fashion. "The neighborhood gossip has got around. I fear you might have to disabuse them of quite a number of notions."

"Indeed? Might I inquire of what I have been accused?" He pressed his hand to his chest and feigned a look of innocence.

"We were told of your heroism in battle in France," Miss Camelford said. Thankfully, she did not bat her eyes.

"I can hardly claim that to be falsehood." The corner of his mouth lifted in a half-grin.

"I have been told you were a crack shot, but have not a taste for venison, so you assume poor skill to avoid having it on your table." Miss Audeley cocked her head and lifted an eyebrow.

Darcy snickered.

"That is far from the most intriguing gossip that has ever got around. But perhaps I should disabuse you of a few of these ideas. Pray excuse us." He tipped his head toward Elizabeth, and led the young ladies toward the center of the room.

Elizabeth stepped a little closer. "I can tell your thoughts by the look in your eye. You do not have to ask. He inquired if there were any suitable young ladies in attendance tonight and requested I make introductions."

"I hardly suspected anything else."

"You are far more obvious than you realize."

"Yet you are very patient with me, and with my family, who it seems are more apt to talk with you than with me."

She pressed her shoulder to his. "Yes, I am, my dear, and yes they are; you would not have it any other way. I am quite certain the prattle of young ladies—and those not so young—would drive you to distraction very quickly. Will you call our guests to dinner?"

"Only if I may have the privilege of escorting you to the dining room."

"I suppose I can suffer that." Her left eye twitched in something not exactly a wink, but still somewhat saucy. How did she do that and still remain so proper?

He called the guests for dinner and they proceeded to the dining room.

THE DINING ROOM was exactly as Elizabeth had imagined it would be. Mouth-watering aromas from the dinner table beckoned everyone to their seats. In the daylight, the large dining room felt a mite overwhelming, even a little stern, but by the warm glow of candles, it transformed into another room entirely.

Crystal and silver glittered from the table, inviting the candlelight to play. The flickering light answered and danced along each place, dodging bits of greenery that had been laid in its path for sport.

Darcy seated Elizabeth at the head of the table and took his place at the foot. Lady Catherine sat beside Darcy, which was unfortunate for him, but hardly avoidable. She was the ranking female in attendance and the place was hers by right. Her face was creased in disagreeable lines—but that was not unusual since Darcy refused to put Sir Jasper out of Pemberley on the basis of his pedigree alone. At least her manners were reliable enough that she would hold her peace until only family were present.

Fitzwilliam seated his new acquaintances on either side of him; Anne took a seat beside one of them and Sir Jasper beside Anne. As annoyed as she was with Fitzwilliam, why was she sitting so close to him? Pray she did not want to find reason to criticize him to Miss Audeley. She could not be that cross, could she?

Elizabeth announced the dishes on the table and waved in the footmen bearing a whole roast pig, a goose, and a haunch of venison. One of those alone would have sufficed at Longbourn. But with so many people at the table tonight, and so many Twelfth Night pies to be made from the leftovers, it seemed the right amount. Sir Graham, Miss Camelford's father, sat beside her. He was largely deaf and content to satisfy his substantial appetite and watch those around him rather than converse. Elizabeth followed his lead and studied Fitzwilliam and his company.

Sir Jasper served Anne's plate, talking all the while. Anne seemed to enjoy his conversation, smiling demurely at what was probably intended to be a joke, but seemed really a rather cruel criticism of his cousin Wharton. Did he realize his was the kind of voice that could be heard clearly from across the table?

Anne hung off every word, almost but not quite fawning. Odd, how she kept glancing at Fitzwilliam, though. What was she about? Seeking his approval?

Fitzwilliam chatted merrily with Miss Audeley. She responded with an appropriate level of decorum and enthusiasm. She was a sweet girl, well-informed, and with just enough fortune to be acceptable to the Matlock family. Perhaps they would find each other pleasing company. But if not, no one's expectations had been raised—at least not yet—so there was no harm done.

Elizabeth rang a crystal bell, and the servants brought in the second course, equally impressive to the first. The menu was exactly what Lady Anne had planned for one of her Christmas dinners, so hopefully, none would find fault. She turned to her left, turning the table to converse with their other dinner partner. How convenient, or was it ironic, that Mr. Audeley had lost his voice that morning and was little able to manage a conversation. Since he did not actually own land and could not hunt, he was content to enjoy the rare treat of a very great deal of venison on his plate, leaving Elizabeth free to continue her observations.

Fitzwilliam appeared to enjoy a lively conversation with Miss Camelford at least as much as the one he had shared with Miss Audeley. It seemed that Miss Camelford's disposition and sharp sense of humor were more complimentary to Fitzwilliam than Miss Audeley's. But that was not for her to decide nor would anyone hear that opinion from her.

Did Anne not like the piece of pie she just tasted? That expression was telling—of something, but it was difficult to discern what. Elizabeth half-closed her eyes, listening carefully.

"Your cousin seems a very gallant gentleman." Miss Audeley took a dainty bite of goose.

Anne shrugged, scowling.

"He mentioned that you were good friends as children. I imagine that was very pleasing, to have such a friend. I am an only child, and my cousins are all much older than I."

"Being an only child is not so much of a trial."

That is hardly what Anne had been telling them for the last fortnight.

Miss Audeley sipped her wine, still trying to smile. The girl really had a stern constitution. "Can you tell me of the colonel's interests? The diversions he enjoys? Does he, for example play cards? Is he a great reader, or does he prefer sport?"

Anne wrinkled her nose. "I suppose I could, but do you not think it a useful conversation in and of itself for you to ask such things of him yourself?"

"Forgive my intrusiveness. I only thought, well, never mind. I see that I have unsettled you in some way. I beg your pardon, Miss de Bourgh." Miss Audeley turned her attention to her plate.

How insupportably rude! What had come over Anne? Was she jealous that there were other eligible young ladies in attendance tonight? She had promised she would not be, but even the best of intentions might not withstand the realities of a situation. Still though, it was incumbent upon a lady to be gracious and polite under such circumstances. Perhaps Anne was not as ready for society as she thought.

Anne sniffed and lifted her chin. How like her mother she looked. She would definitely not appreciate that observation.

Elizabeth caught Darcy's eye. He nodded just enough for her to notice. She rang the bell, and the servants began their elaborate dance, clearing the tablecloth, placing the sweet course and extinguishing candles.

Darcy had dared wonder aloud at the need for such pageantry. But heavens, it was the Christmas pudding! There could hardly be too much pageantry and drama. It had to be like the Harlequin in the pantos he so enjoyed—impossible to overlook or forget.

Two footmen stood in the doorway, bearing a large platter with the huge cannonball shaped pudding between them. They lowered it for Mrs. Reynolds to light the brandy. Blue flames enveloped the pudding, filling the dining room with a distinct flickering glow, the color of the Christmas feast.

The footmen paraded it around the table, ensuring all the guests an excellent view of the spectacle. Finally, they deposited it at the head of the table.

Georgiana and the other young ladies at the table applauded softly. How dear they were and so easy to please. Clearly Lady Catherine did not approve of their display, but she was not Pemberley's arbiter of acceptable behavior. Lucky for them all. Heartfelt joy and appreciation would always be welcome here, whatever form they took.

The brandy-blue fames faded, replaced by the familiar glow of many wax candles while the footmen hurried to distribute slices of the pudding.

Elizabeth snuck a quick glance at Darcy as he savored the first bite. He closed his eyes as a faraway expression painted his features. Yes! They had succeeded at recreating his boyhood puddings! Her eyes misted. It was a silly matter to be so moved by, but there it was.

"Oh!"

The charms were being found.

"You found the ring!" Anne cried.

What ring? Elizabeth jumped. How was that possible?

Sir Jasper held a little pewter ring aloft on his little finger, to the admiration of Anne and the others around them.

Darcy stared at Elizabeth wide-eyed. She shook her head. The Darcy charms were silver, not pewter. Her eyes narrowed, and she caught Sir Jasper's gaze.

Arrogant fellow only smiled and winked at her. But guilt was written in all his features. That he even thought to manufacture such an occurrence! It was an action worthy of Mr. Wickham. Her stomach churned. Despicable man.

Anne flashed her a stern look. She offered one in return. They both returned to their puddings, though Elizabeth's had suddenly lost all flavor.

"Pray, ladies, would you join me in the drawing room?" Elizabeth rose. Perhaps it was a bit early, but she could not share a table with that man one moment longer.

She led the ladies out, Lady Catherine at her elbow. What joy was hers. She clenched her jaw.

"How could you allow—" Lady Catherine hissed through her teeth, not looking at Elizabeth.

"How can I control a matter of chance? Perhaps you should have ensured you found that charm yourself had you been so concerned for the outcome."

She increased her pace, leaving Lady Catherine sputtering in her wake.

Disagreeable though Anne could be, she was nothing—absolutely nothing—to her mother.

A tea service and biscuits were waiting for their leisure in the evergreen-draped large drawing room.

"Might Anne and I play?" Georgiana asked, eyes wide and innocent.

Did she really think that Elizabeth did not see through her ruse to avoid playing for a larger audience? No doubt a mix of maidenly modesty, shyness, and a desire to allow Anne to have center stage for her 'come out' as it were. "Please do."

As they played, Elizabeth circulated among her guests, all uniformly complimentary and gracious, as proper ladies always were in the company of their hostess. What they would say behind Elizabeth's back remained to be seen.

"Elizabeth." Anne appeared at her shoulder.

When had they stopped playing?

"May I speak to you for a moment?"

"Of course." Elizabeth followed her to an unoccupied corner between two large curio cabinets.

Anne worried her hands together. "I am sorry to bring this up now, after all you have done for me to make this evening truly special and memorable. I do so appreciate everything, truly I do. But I cannot hold my tongue on such a matter of great import."

Thank heavens! She realized Sir Jasper's nature and would not need—

"Those women you introduced to Fitzwilliam—"

"Miss Camelford and Miss Audeley?"

"More to the point, Miss Thinks-Too-Well-of-Herself and Miss Has-no-Good-Connections-of-her-Own."

Elizabeth edged back, eyes wide. "Excuse me? You are speaking of—"

"Your friends? Truly? You cannot see their motives? I am shocked, positively shocked that you would consider either of them appropriate to admit into his acquaintance. If I did not know you better, I would think you some kind of horrid matchmaker in cahoots with them. Neither of those girls is worthy of him." Anne's face turned positively florid.

Upset she might be, but she would learn what her mother had. "Then I imagine you have little to be concerned for. If they are as you say, he is possessed of adequate discernment and strength of character to discontinue their acquaintance with him."

"He is under pressure from his family to marry, and if he believes those ninnies have the Darcy approbation, he might indeed be snared. It would be the greatest kindness for them all if you would discreetly mention his family's disapproval to those girls."

"His family?"

"You cannot imagine my mother approves."

She could not imagine Lady Catherine had even noticed.

"If you are their friend, you will set their expectations appropriately."

Elizabeth opened her mouth, but no words formed.

"Thank you so much, I knew you would understand." Anne took Elizabeth's hands, squeezed them hard and faded back into the drawing room..

Chapter 8

December 30, 1813

SEVERAL MORNINGS LATER, Fitzwilliam hurried to the morning room. Someone had made a mistake—at least according to his valet—and his society pages had been delivered with the newspaper to Darcy's place in the morning room.

Granted, a servant would shoulder the blame for those pages appearance, not him—but still that was hardly fair. Not to mention, it might make it far more difficult for him to acquire them in the future, and Anne desperately needed the education they would provide, especially now.

Fortune smiled on him! Darcy was nowhere to be seen and the room was totally empty! Not even coffee or tea had been brought in.

He rifled through the papers at Darcy's place and

removed the gossip pages. Breathing more easily, he sat opposite Darcy's chair and settled in to read, quickly, before Darcy arrived. The usual suspects, the usual antics—wait—this was different. A Sir P. from Derbyshire—damn the writers for trying to obfuscate just enough to be difficult when one really needed to know what was going on. He slapped the paper with the back of two fingers. Drunkenness at a party ... in the company of multiple ladybirds, what debauchery might have taken place? ... gambling for very high stakes ... hints of ruin, but nothing, no one definite.

Heavy foot falls echoed in the hall. No servant would dare walk so loudly. Fitzwilliam jumped and tucked his papers into his coat. "Good morning, Darcy."

Mrs. Reynolds scurried in behind him, a pot of coffee in hand. She poured him a cup and set it at his place before he even sat down. "Sir?" She looked at Fitzwilliam.

"Yes." A cup of his own appeared. "So, have you rested enough now that you can think about the Twelfth Night ball?"

"Already on to the next event? Are you not unable to savor the pleasures of the first? I am quite certain Mrs. Darcy's Christmas dinner compared favorably to any Mother hosted."

"It was a memorable event and a very fitting way for Elizabeth to establish her reputation as a hostess." There were a few bits that could have used some improvement, but it would not do to express that to Darcy now.

"Poor Elizabeth was utterly spent the days after. I am not sure she left her rooms at all for two days complete. I am a mite concerned—"

"Pish-posh man, I swear you worry for sport. It was not just Elizabeth. I saw nothing of Anne or Georgiana, or even Aunt Catherine those two days, either." It was a relaxing, easy pair of days, not having to keep watch over Anne and her suitors.

Darcy twitched his head and picked up his paper and scanned through it. Did he really read that fast, or was he just looking for specific information?

Mrs. Reynolds appeared again, this time with letters on a silver salver. Elizabeth followed on her heels, with a countenance as lively as the morning sunshine.

Darcy brightened for a moment and took the letters. Then his scowl said it all; these were the letters he had been waiting for.

"Pray excuse me. There is urgent business I must attend." Darcy escorted Elizabeth to her seat and left.

"You seem well-rested at last," Fitzwilliam said.

"Thank you. I am glad to at least have that appearance. None of the events at Longbourn were quite so elaborate. The differences in scale are noteworthy." She reached for her sewing basket.

"I can imagine, but be assured I heard nothing but compliments from your guests."

"You are too kind, but I know people too well to believe that. Every society has its scolds and curmudgeons, even this one."

Fitzwilliam chuckled, probably exactly as she intended. "But everyone knows they are not to be attended to—even here."

"So I gather you enjoyed yourself and found the company agreeable?"

"Very much so." He winked.

Would Elizabeth be amused at the conversation he

had with Anne yesterday when she had declared his two new acquaintances simpering ninnies? Who knew Anne could be so severe upon her own sex—but indeed she was. Perhaps it was only in revenge for his disapproval of her suitors. It would not be unlike her.

Still though, she did have a few good points in her arguments. Perhaps neither of them was truly suitable. He would have to observe them more closely the next time they were in company. That is where he and Anne were different—he could take opinions and advice without taking offense.

Something in Elizabeth's expression— "Did Anne complain to you—"

Elizabeth looked down demurely.

"Pray pay no attention to her. As much as I am her friend, I do not forget that she is indeed her mother's daughter and will find fault with anyone and anything simply because she can."

Elizabeth fixed her eyes on her sewing. "Does she know you say such things of her?"

"I cannot hazard a guess, but I prefer that she did not."

Elizabeth sniggered behind her hand.

Mrs. Reynolds appeared in the doorway, again. Did she do anything but lurk about waiting to pop into the morning room? "Excuse me. The master would see the Colonel in his study."

Fitzwilliam jumped, nearly spilling his coffee. "Pray excuse me, Elizabeth."

She looked concerned, but asked nothing. Which was good as he had nothing to tell—not yet.

He all but ran to the study. Darcy waited at the door and closed it firmly.

"And? What is the word?"

Darcy fell into his seat. "The news is worse than I imagined. My acquaintance tells me he attended the card party in which Sir Jasper bet his family seat in a game of Vingt-et un and lost it. It seems he is desperately in search of sufficient cash to purchase it back. He was given until the end of January to do so. One can only assume his interest in Anne is—"

"Interest only in her fortune and in Rosings, which no doubt he would gamble away at the very first opportunity."

"Even if he got Rosings Park back for the de Bourgh family, there seems little chance it would remain in the family long enough to be passed to another generation." He handed Fitzwilliam the letter.

He scanned it and muttered under his breath. There were some oaths that even Darcy did not need to hear. "How am I going to tell Anne? She did not take my recommendations for caution well."

"I had thought to invite my acquaintance to Pemberley and allow him to deliver the information first hand." Darcy raked his hair back from his forehead.

"Can you not just pitch Sir Jasper out of the back door? It would be far simpler and much more satisfying. I would be very happy to assist you."

"Be that as it may, his kind—and his cousins—are likely to see reports of such treatment make it into the society pages. I cannot do that to Elizabeth. It would reflect very badly on her."

"She does not deserve that. Invite your acquaintance then. I suppose, I must try to break the news to Anne and, at the very least, try to keep her away from Sir Jasper's machinations until he arrives."

January 1, 1814

Early on New Year's Day, Fitzwilliam made his way down to the morning room. There was something about the start of a new year that demanded rising early and reflecting upon what had been and what might be. It might be a custom unique to him, but New Year's Day would not be right without it.

He sat near the windows that pulled in the morning light—sunrise was fading into morning. Fresh flowers had not yet been placed in the vases. Yesterday's—last year's really—marigolds were a touch faded and limp. A fire had been lit, but obviously not long ago, the air still carried a sharp chill—not entirely unpleasant, more invigorating. And far better than waking up in a tent on a French plain.

Mrs. Reynolds appeared briefly to place a steaming mug of coffee on the table near him. She was truly a treasure. Luckily, Darcy understood that. He wrapped his hands around the mug until it just burned—hot, dark and bitter.

What a year it had been. With Anne going off to school, his brother contemplating—seriously this time—taking a wife, Darcy navigating his first year of marriage, and his own sell-out from the army, how many things were changing around him? Selling out had not been an easy decision, but he had seen enough battle, enough death, enough blood. Mother had said he looked old beyond his years. He certainly felt that way. His allowance, and the money from his sell-out—if he was careful—could keep him comfortable—not in the style to which he had been accustomed, but comfortable—and if he took up Darcy's invitation to live at Pemberley, then he might be more than comfortable. It was something to consider.

If nothing else, it might allow him to further his acquaintances with Miss Camelford and Miss Audeley. By no means was he violently in love, nor, hopefully, were they, but they were agreeable enough to consider seeing more of them.

"Good morning." Elizabeth entered, with Mrs. Reynolds bearing a pot of tea just a step behind.

He rose and pulled her chair out for her. "So where is your lord and master? I am surprised he is not already here."

"He went straight to his office this morning. He and the steward are meeting to discuss spring planting and improvements."

"Does he never stop working?"

Elizabeth lifted a very teasing eyebrow. "He has been known to."

He nearly choked on his sip of coffee.

"And it is just as well he is occupied this morning." She removed folded papers from her sewing basket. "As I thought you wished to discuss these. Quite informative."

The society pages he had asked her to read.

He leaned forward, elbow on the table. "That would be one word to describe them. Perhaps not the one I would have chosen ..."

"I am sure not. No doubt you would have something far more colorful in mind. I certainly did."

"So what do you think? Have I hope of getting Anne's attention with those?"

"I have been giving it a great deal of thought—what is that?" She dropped the papers and turned toward the window.

Laughter and shrieking—happy not threatening sounds, female and young—outside, near the well.

It was New Year's Day!

"Damn foolish girls. They are creaming the well." He ran for the back door, Elizabeth following.

Where had Anne got that idea? No one in her family practiced that Scottish tradition. Daft woman was trying to encourage Sir Jasper to propose—and that was simply not going to happen.

Anne and Miss Gifford, both barefoot and without a proper shawl to boot, had just made it to the well directly behind the kitchen, both scrambling to draw the first water from it. Whether more aggressive or more determined, Anne managed to secure the first bucketful.

"Dare I wonder who you will be offering a glass to?" Miss Gifford leaned on Anne's shoulder.

"No, you may not." He stormed up to them. "Both of you get back to the house and get proper clothes on! You will certainly catch your death of cold like that. Go, go both of you." He shooed them along like a sheepdog herding recalcitrant lambs.

Miss Gifford ducked her head and scurried inside.

"You sound like my old governess. What has come over you? You used to be able to have fun. Why are you so insistent on ruining ours?" She watched the door through which her friend had disappeared.

"Have you any idea how ridiculous it is for you to be out barefoot in such weather? Since when has risking your health and well-being been considered having fun? Or is that to be a new parlor game for the evening?"

"Leave me alone, Fitzwilliam. No one has put you in charge of me."

He grasped her upper arm and guided her—forcefully—into the kitchen. "We need to talk."

From the corner of his eye, he watched Elizabeth slip back behind a partition in the kitchen. Probably just as well that she witnessed this; she could testify on his behalf when Lady Catherine complained he had not done enough to separate Anne from her suitor.

"I do not want to talk to you. I do not care what you have to say." Anne pulled away from his grasp and stood near the large fireplace.

"You should."

"Why? You are just a lackey for my mother. I want no part of anything she has to say."

"I am not and have never been. I am your friend. You must listen to me." He grasped her shoulders and shook her.

"Stop that, you will make me spill my water."

He grabbed the bucket, sloshing them both. Blast it all, that water was icy cold. "The last thing you need is this water." He lifted the bucket and drank from it, allowing it to spill down his chest. The bucket empty, he cast it aside so violently it struck the fireplace hearth and bounced on the stone floor several times.

"What have you done? That was for Sir Jasper, not you." Anne looked like she had lost something of real value.

"What I have always done, what is best for you whether you realize it or not."

"I never asked for that favor, and I certainly do not want it now." She tried to turn away, but he held her shoulders firm.

"I do not care what you want. I know what you need right now. You must listen to me. I absolutely insist."

"If I listen, will you let me go? I am wet because of you, and now I am cold. I want to be warm and dry."

"Listen then and I will release you."

She folded her arms over her chest, shivering just a bit—probably for effect. "Speak."

"Darcy and I have been looking into Sir Jasper. He is not what he has put himself out to be. His affairs are not as he has represented them to you."

"If you mean he has debts, I am aware of them. He has been entirely forthcoming in that regard."

"I doubt it. Where has he told you his debts come from?"

"Crops that failed, tenants that did not pay their rent. Even you can hardly fault him for that." She looked so smug—unbearably so.

"He is a liar, and not even a good one."

"Do not slander him!"

"What do you call a man who has lost his family seat to a hand of cards and only pursues a woman because she has the means to permit him to buy it back?"

"Those are lies!" She stamped—that must have hurt against the cold stone. "I cannot believe it. I will not. He is a good man, and he cares for me, more than you do. He would not deceive me."

"And I would? When have I ever done such a thing?"

"You are in league with my mother. What more is there to know? You will do anything to make her happy—just like everyone else. What has she offered you to buy your favor? I am sure your assistance has not come cheaply—or has our friendship meant so little to you that it has?"

"Enough! I have discharged my duty. I will not hear any more of your foolishness and insults. I do not deserve this, and I will not tolerate it." He threw up his hands and stormed from the kitchen. Warm dry clothes and distance from that infuriating woman would be most welcome at this point.

ELIZABETH HELD HER breath and balled her fists. Contrary, foolish girl. She had no more sense than Lydia!

"What are you looking at, you stupid cow! Get away from me!" Anne shrieked.

A terrified scullery maid ran past Elizabeth.

First she abused Fitzwilliam, her most faithful friend in the world. Now, she was abusing Pemberley's staff? Enough was certainly enough.

Elizabeth drew in a deep breath and pulled back her shoulders. This was not a time for an angry older sister; for this she must be Mistress of Pemberley.

Slowly, deliberately she strode out from behind the partition and stepped toe to toe with a very startled Anne, face flushed in the heat of the large fireplace.

"What do you want?" Anne's lip curled back, and she narrowed her eyes.

Oh, no, she would not win at that game. "What are you doing in my kitchen? One does not customarily find guests standing barefoot and wet in one's kitchen, interfering with the efforts of the staff."

"I do not need this right now. Leave me alone. Can you not see I am upset enough already?" She planted her hands on her hips and leaned close to Elizabeth's face.

Elizabeth matched her stance. "You are a guest in my home. It does not behoove you to give me orders."

"You are mistress of Pemberley, I understand that. We all here understand. You do not need to lord your triumph over me. Or have you suddenly taken to gloating."

"You are a fool. Utterly and totally. Even more so than I had ever suspected."

"Who are you to judge me? Get out of my way, and leave me alone." She tried to step around Elizabeth, skidding slightly in the puddle Fitzwilliam had left, but Elizabeth cut her off.

"No. You will listen to what I have to say."

"And if I do not want to?"

"You will listen any way. Not just Fitzwilliam, but Darcy and everyone else in the house has been trying to be patient and kind with you. You have repaid us with temper tantrums, insults and worse. Now you are ready to throw yourself away on a cad worse than the one my sister wed simply because you are too proud and too headstrong to listen to anyone."

"What are you talking about?" Anne's expression shifted. Perhaps Elizabeth had got her attention.

"Your precious Sir Jasper is a bounder! A rake! He only cares for your fortune, nothing for you. He wants Rosings, but not for the de Bourgh family, but to buy back his own seat without consideration or care for you or your mother."

"I know he has debts. What gentleman does not? Except for Darcy of course, I understand he is perfect. You are exaggerating his situation far out of proportion."

"And you are ignoring the danger you are in. Here, look at this." Elizabeth shoved the society pages in her hand, pointing to a section she had marked in pencil.

"Sir P? Who is Sir P? You cannot imagine this is Sir Jasper?"

"You know the gossips are apt to use initials—"

"This is not him. I am certain of it." Anne paused and read the section, tracing the words with her finger. "Apparently Fitzwilliam is better intentioned than I gave him credit for, but he is still very, very wrong."

"With so much at stake, why would you ignore the counsel of your oldest, most faithful friend, and your family in favor of a man whom you barely know? You are a far greater fool than even my sister was, and I am sorry for you. Profoundly and deeply sorry. But pray, do not ask any more favors of me. I am done doing them for an ungrateful girl-woman who will not even try to be a rational creature. You can only hope your friend Fitzwilliam will be more understanding when you realize the depth of your folly, for I can hardly imagine Miss Gifford will be of much use to you then."

Anne's face turned several shades of red and sputtered something very unladylike. She stomped out, kicking the discarded bucket as she passed.

Elizabeth pressed her temples hard. Was this what her parents had dealt with in raising five daughters? If it was, pray she would only bear Darcy sons.

January 4, 1814

AFTER THEIR LAST encounter, Anne seemed to keep to herself. She did deign to come to dinner, whether not to offend Elizabeth, or to avoid Darcy's or her Mother's scoldings, it was difficult to tell. But she did excuse herself early from the drawing room afterward, and had little interest in any of the evening amusements.

It should have given Fitzwilliam some peace of mind not to have to watch the flirtation between her and Sir Jasper. Should have—but it did not.

Everything about the situation felt wrong and dangerous, pinging his nerves like over-tightened violin strings, ready to snap at the slightest provocation. Almost like being back in France, waiting, watching, and expecting the enemy behind any corner.

Yes, it was a good thing he had sold out.

By the third day, his skin crawled, and he paced and patrolled the house, snapping at everyone around him. Perhaps that was why Georgiana and Miss Gifford suddenly decided to pay a call upon Miss Roberts. The way Georgiana had glared at him when she informed him that not only would they be gone, but the men had gone out riding for the day, almost as if she was accusing him of driving them all from the house.

Stuff and nonsense! Darcy and Elizabeth were still there and did not seem bothered, so if the others were, that was distinctly their problem and not his.

He paced through the family wing. It was quiet, as it should be. All the ancestor's portraits gazed down at him solemnly, but there was a certain demand in their eyes. What did they want from him?

He continued down the guest wing. Quiet as a tomb, as it was said, with his footsteps echoing off the walls.

Surely there was nothing wrong. Yet, his nerves would not settle. If he did not get them settled soon, he would surely run mad. Perhaps a drink. Darcy had an excellent French brandy in his study. Surely he would not begrudge Fitzwilliam some.

He trotted down the grand marble staircase.

Oh, the trouble he and Darcy had got into on this staircase as boys. The stairs were wide enough for three or four to walk abreast, wide enough for a small carpet to glide over the stairs. What a wild ride that had been! Uncle Darcy had not agreed with them though, and saw to it they would consider it a bad option ever after. Still it had been jolly good fun.

He paused at the first landing. Music? Yes, it was. Anne's playing—from the music room? Perhaps she would talk with him now? Then again, she might simply storm off as she had the last time he had tried. Best test her mood first.

He probably should not do it, but he ducked into the servants' door and toward the door in the music room. Technically it was spying on her—another favorite game he and Darcy had indulged in during their boyhood—but it was for Anne's comfort, and yes, his own as well. Surely that elevated the act away from just childish bad manners, did it not?

He peeked through the servants' door into the music room, opened it just a hair, just enough to see Anne at the piano. She still wore a plain morning dress, had not bothered to dress for the day or even curl her hair. That spoke volumes, but what did it say? Her cheeks were pale and drawn—had she been sleeping? Clearly she was upset, but at whom?

She stopped playing and looked around, a soft smile blossoming.

Hell and damnation, Sir Jasper was standing at the door. He sauntered in and closed it behind him.

The hair on the back of Fitzwilliam's neck stood. His fists balled into tight knots. It had been a long time since he had used them—but not long enough that he had forgotten how.

"You would make a very sweet painting there at the piano, in your morning gown. I would hang such a work in my home with pride, though perhaps a painting in dishabille might be even more appealing."

Anne blushed and smiled at him.

How dare he be so familiar with her!

He approached, slow and smooth. "It seems like you have been avoiding me the last few days. I have missed your company. Very much."

"With all the diversions of Pemberley, I cannot imagine my presence makes any difference at all." She shrugged and looked away.

"Why have you been hiding from me, my dear Anne." He caressed the top of the pianoforte.

His dear Anne? Fitzwilliam ground his teeth.

"It is difficult to know what to think." She bit her lip.

"Has that dreadful cousin of yours been slandering me again?" He drummed his fingers along the piano.

"Do not speak of him so."

Did she really say that?

"Why such devotion to a man who cares nothing of your happiness?"

Anne pulled wrinkled, dingy papers out from behind her music. "Tell me about this."

"Society pages! Piffle and bother. Utter nonsense that is not to be trusted." He tossed them to the floor.

"But why did they write such things about you?"

"Me? Why would you say that is me? How do you know? Or have the Darcys told you so?"

"Do you say it is not? Look me in the eyes, and tell me that it is not."

"Will you believe me then if I do?"

Anne opened her mouth to speak, but said nothing.

"If you will not, then why should I bother denying it? Why should I say anything at all? My own testimony is not good enough for you? You would much rather believe those who are trying to ruin me?" His faced knotted in a threatening mien.

"I said nothing of the kind."

"I thought you cared for me, that we were close to some kind of understanding. It wounds me to think I was so very mistaken. You are no different to other women I have known in society." He turned aside and pressed his hand to his chest.

Manipulating bounder!

"How can you say that about me?" Anne stood and turned to face him. "You know I am not like that."

He avoided her gaze. "I feel as though I hardly know you now at all."

"That is too cruel. Do not say such things. You know me very well."

He turned suddenly and took her hands in his. "Then stop this foolishness, dear, sweet Anne of mine. Consent to be my wife and come away with me."

She edged half a step back, stammering.

"Do not deny me or you will be the worst flirt, the most despicable tease in all of England." He lunged, pulling her close, and kissed her forcefully.

Fitzwilliam tensed, but hesitated.

Anne pushed hard against his chest. "No! Stop—let me go!"

He grabbed at her again, ripping her bodice.

Fitzwilliam plunged through the door, snarling like a wild cat, blind to everything but Sir Jasper. He threw his arm around Jasper's neck and tightened his elbow around it, adding his other hand to his wrist for leverage. A little backward pressure forced Jasper to release Anne, who crumpled to the ground.

Fitzwilliam threw Jasper to the carpet. He screamed with his first unencumbered breath, as Fitzwilliam's fists rained down upon his chest. Jasper threw up his arms to shield himself, but to little avail. Clearly the man had never fought to save his own life, much less that of another.

The door flew open and banged against the wall.

"What is going on?" Darcy boomed, his voice carrying all the authority of a general.

Several footmen stopped near Fitzwilliam but hesitated to put their hands on him. Smart, probably saved themselves injury that way. He pushed himself up, controlling the urge to kick Jasper in the ribs. The footmen rushed in to restrain the bruised and bleeding baronet.

Fitzwilliam dashed to Anne and helped her to her feet. She clung to him, weeping, her face buried in his shoulder.

Darcy approached. "What happened?"

"Sir Jasper made her an offer of marriage. When she hesitated, he attempted to force her."

Darcy leaned down close to Anne's face. "Is this true?"

She nodded into Fitzwilliam's shoulder.

Darcy whirled on his heel and stalked to Sir Jasper. "You and your cousins have one hour to leave the bounds of Pemberley. If you make any attempt, if there is any mention or even hint of Miss de Bourgh and yourself in any of the society pages, I will see that you are ruined, utterly and completely. Am I understood?"

Fitzwilliam wrapped his arm tightly around Anne. "If you trouble her in any way again, I will personally see to it that you will forever regret your actions. Never let her see your face again."

"My men will see to your departure. Do not permit him out of your sight and send two riders to escort them off the estate. Follow them all the way to Lambton. Send someone to find Wharton and Sadler and get them out of here as well." Darcy dismissed them with a wave of his hand.

The footmen escorted Sir Jasper out.

Darcy touched Anne's elbow. "I will fetch Elizabeth."

Anne lifted her head. "Pray do not tell my mother."

"She need know nothing about this." Fitzwilliam caught Darcy's eye.

He nodded sharply and left.

"Are you injured?" Fitzwilliam pulled her closer again, as much to assure himself of her safety as for her comfort.

"I do not think so. Where were you? How did you come so quickly?"

"You will not like it." He chuckled softly. Yes, it

was a little forced, but a touch of levity was necessary. "I was in the servants' passage."

"Why?"

"I wanted to talk to you, but did not know if you would receive me. I hid there to try to discern your mood."

"Have I truly been that awful to you?" She peered up at him.

"I am thankful you did not encourage that bounder, that you did not accept his offer. I am proud of you that you made the decision to trust what I had told you, even though you did not like what I had to say."

"And that is what you heard in all of that." Her eyes shimmered.

"Do you wish to correct me?"

She sniffled and choked back a sob. A strangled cry broke free, and she shuddered in his arms. He pressed her close and rubbed her back.

Pray Elizabeth would know what to do to comfort her, but at least now she was safe and content with his friendship once again.

Chapter 9

THE NEXT TWO days threw Pemberley into a frenzy, the likes of which Darcy had never seen. Miss Gifford had been, not unexpectedly, distressed at the dismissal of her cousins from Pemberley. What Darcy had not anticipated was the amount of noise and commotion one upset young woman could produce in the halls of his home. The fury only became worse when Anne stepped in to try to explain to her friend what had actually happened.

Being a good sort of girl who could hardly believe ill of her relations, she decried the slander of her cousin and insisted she and her companion would leave immediately as well. Darcy offered to send a rider ahead of them to try to find and inform Sir Jasper's party of their departure and a pair of men to accompany their party until they could join with her cousins. Thankfully, those offers were accepted, and

Darcy could see them off with a clear conscience as to their safety. That it enabled them to depart somewhat sooner was a happy side effect.

Explaining the affair to Aunt Catherine without divulging the actual nature of Sir Jasper's transgressions proved less difficult than Darcy feared. She was so pleased that Sir Jasper and all his despicable family were leaving that she never bothered to ask what finally moved Darcy to throw him out, although she made certain to complain it had taken too long.

The next day, the day before the ball, on the suggestion of Mrs. Darcy, he invited Fitzwilliam to spend the day hunting and leave the house and all the preparations to those more equipped to handle them. Perhaps not the most politic way to put it all, but she was correct, and they were both only too happy for the contemplation the woods offered. Fitzwilliam was uncharacteristically quiet the entire hunt, which was a bit unusual, but no doubt, being forced to physically restrain Sir Jasper weighed on him. That evening, the ladies all took dinner trays in their rooms, and the whole party retired early in anticipation of the final push the next day.

Without the drama offered by Anne's—now former—friends, the final flurry of ball preparations proved quite tolerable, even a bit intriguing as the house slowly transformed into a fanciful, mythical setting. Normal paintings were changed out for images from folklore, both local and classical—had Georgiana and Anne drawn those? Some were really quite good. Soft swags of fabric hid bookcases and curio cabinets, erasing elements of the everyday. In the ballroom, two artists worked diligently, chalking the floor with the fully drawn images of the night sky's constellations. By evening Pemberley was a different, wondrous place indeed. Mother would have been proud.

Just before the first guests were set to arrive, Darcy knocked on Elizabeth's dressing room door. She had been so gracious as to excuse him from fancy dress that night—nothing could overcome his abhorrence of it, especially after Lady Matlock's Twelfth Night ball two years ago. The mark cousin Letty had left on his psyche might well be indelible. That did not keep him from anticipating seeing Elizabeth in her fancy dress, though.

Her lady's maid opened the door for him. He stepped in and gasped.

She stood in the center of the room, bathed in a mix of fire and candlelight, warm and flickering, wrapped in the exotic blue and purple saree. Gold threads in the silk glittered, surrounding her in a glow nearly divine. Her hair, held back from her face with elaborate pins and ribbons, cascaded in curls down her back.

"Have I your approval sir?" She smiled—half-shy, half-enticing.

He ran his fingers around the inside of his cravat. "I am not certain I should permit you out of this room, Mrs. Darcy. Should other men have the privilege of seeing you thus?"

She flushed brightly, and looked down. Trying to be demure now? No, that was simply more teasing on her part. Utterly delightful.

He stepped closer and held her shoulders. "I try not to be a jealous man, my dear, but tonight may be very, very difficult. Would I be selfish if I ask that you dance with no one but me?"

She rose on tiptoes and kissed his cheek. "I would be happy to oblige you."

Best not tell her that he would not have permitted her to leave her room had she not agreed.

Elizabeth glowed in a way he had never seen before as he escorted her down the great stairs. It was a shame there was not an audience to receive her as they descended. But it did mean he kept her to himself just a little while longer, and that was not a bad thing.

Fitzwilliam and Aunt Catherine waited for them in the transformed drawing room, every bit as fantastical a place as the ballroom. A nymph, or perhaps Pan himself might jump out at them from any corner. How had she managed it?

"You have truly outdone yourself tonight, Elizabeth. Everything is as stunning as our hostess." Fitzwilliam grinned saucily—exactly in the way that he knew would most provoke Darcy.

But tonight nothing was going to provoke him, not even Aunt Catherine's mutterings from the corner about why Elizabeth had chosen something foreign to wear. Was something English not good enough?

Guests arrived and the drawing room was filled with swans, princesses, knights, and—was that someone playing at Napoleon? Hopefully it would not incite Fitzwilliam. Somehow all the odd characters seemed to fit in the fantasy world that Elizabeth had created.

She glanced at him. It was time. He signaled Fitzwilliam who hurried upstairs.

FITZWILLIAM DRESSED AS an English courtier—a few visits to used clothes sellers and rifling through the attics at Matlock had produced a quite passable fancy dress with little strain on his purse. How fitting a garb it was for him while escorting Georgiana into the ball.

He knocked on her door, and she appeared swathed in white gauzy stuff, wispy, with wings and feathers. Her hair was done up in flowers and pearl headed pins. She was every bit the fairy she had hoped to be.

"You will be the talk of the evening, my dear, in all the right ways. Will you allow me to conduct you to your ball?" He offered her his arm.

She slipped her hand in the crook of his elbow.

They paused at the top of the stairs. The low crowd noises from below fell silent. Darcy and Elizabeth stood at either side at the base of the stairs, offering silent encouragement. Georgiana squeezed his arm hard and nodded with a bit less certainty.

"No doubt Darcy has already requested the first dance. Might I have the pleasure of one during the evening?" They started down the stairs.

"I would be honored to dance with a courtier." Her voice was a little shaky, but whose would not be at their first ball?

Her friends applauded her entrance and immediately gathered around her as Darcy and Elizabeth began the process of making formal introductions. He stepped back. She was doing well, and looked more relaxed with each one. There was little for him to do right now.

Aunt Catherine appeared at his elbow. Blast it all, the room was too crowded to escape her. "Good evening, Aunt."

"That is your grandfather's wig, you know."

"Really? I thought it had been my grandmother's." He wrapped one of the white curls around his finger and smiled as effeminately as he knew how.

"I need none of your cheek young man." She slapped his shoulder with her fan. Like Darcy, Aunt Catherine had nothing to do with fancy dress, wearing her most elaborate—and rather out of fashion—Chinese silk gown.

"What a shame when I have so much to offer."

"You are trying to vex me." Her face wrinkled into a Rowlandson's caricature of a sour old woman.

He would have to find that print and give a copy to Darcy next Christmastide. For his private enjoyment of course. "Is that not why you came to me, because you were in need of vexation."

She grumbled something low under her breath. "I need you to do something."

Of course she did. "Of what service are you in need?"

"Anne refuses to come out of her room. She cannot afford to miss this event and the opportunities it affords her. She needs to make new acquaintances. The company here in Derbyshire is promising—"

"You mean it is now without de Bourghs." Fitzwilliam crossed his arms over his chest.

"That is one appeal, yes. She is insistent that she will refuse any match I propose. But one that Mrs. Darcy introduces her to might be more acceptable."

"You have already instructed Mrs. Darcy on the introductions you wish her to make—and those she should not."

"That is none of your concern. I need you to bring Anne out of her room and see that she receives those introductions. Go now, and make haste. She should not miss the start of the dancing." She propelled him toward the stairs with the end of her fan.

The woman could brandish that thing like a sword. Poor Anne. After the trauma Sir Jasper had inflicted, it was little surprise she would not be in the mood for company. But perhaps the festivities would help take her mind off things. She did not, after all, have to dance. There was a room set up for cards and games that should be a suitable diversion.

He knocked on her door.

The maid peeked it open. "She does not wish to see anyone, sir."

"I am not anyone. Anne, I am coming in, you had best be presentable." He glanced at the maid for confirmation.

She nodded, eyes wide and losing the color in her face. He shouldered past her and marched into the dressing room.

Dresses, lengths of fabric and sewing paraphernalia littered every dresser, press, chair and even draped the side of the long mirror. Enough candles to light an entire cottage brightened the space. Anne stood, resplendent, in the center of the room, commanding attention from everything and everyone within.

"I told you I do not want company!" She spun to face him, the hem of her rich, red skirt flaring and swirling around her.

"You are stunning." And she was, stopping him in

his tracks. The red complimented her features and the dress, her figure in remarkable ways. "Simply stunning."

"You do not have to say that."

"I know. I would not except that it is true." He walked a full circle around her. "A phoenix?"

"That was the effect I was trying for." Her shrug was listless, even hopeless.

"And you have achieved it." He braced his shoulder on the wall and leaned against it, staring unabashed. "There is a place for all manner of fanciful creatures downstairs you know."

"I am not going."

"So I had heard."

"Then why are you still here?"

"I have been sent to fetch you."

"Tell Mother—"

"No, I am no messenger boy." He pushed away from the wall. "Besides I think she is right. You do no one any good hiding here in your room. You should be at the ball, honoring your cousins and their hospitality in inviting you to attend."

"This is Georgiana's night, not mine. No one needs my presence or will even miss me. And I do not need the reminder that we are going through these motions in order to find husbands to make us all respectable women."

"It is not so bad."

"How would you know? Men are despicable creatures."

"I do not appreciate being included in that remark." He crossed his arms and rocked back on his heels.

She cuffed his shoulder. "I am not talking about

you, you ninny. You are not a man."

"Excuse me? Now you have truly offended me. I dare say there are many who would heartily disagree with you."

She stomped. It was nice to see a little of her fire back. "You know that is not what I meant."

"But it is what you said."

"You are not like them!"

"I am glad you noticed."

"And so did those two addle-pates who will be no doubt hanging off your arms tonight. It is easy for you men. There are pretty women lurking about on every corner. But for women—" She looked him full in the eye. "Where am I going to find a man like you to marry?"

Her eyes were full of fire and challenge, enough to heat his blood and arouse his mind, rare as the phoenix she portrayed. She had always been bold and blunt with him like no other woman had. Shiny bits and bobs applied like beauty marks glittered on her face—it was impossible to look away. Darcy might think her looks rather unremarkable, but had he ever really looked at her?

"There is one, right here before you." He spread open hands toward her.

"Oh do be serious, Fitzwilliam. It is not kind of you to tease me when I am already so vexed."

He took her hand. "I am not teasing you. I have never been so serious with you, ever. We have been very good friends for such a long time. What makes better sense than for us to marry?"

True, he had not actively considered the idea in quite some time, but it was so obvious right now, and so completely right.

Oh the look on her face, at once perplexed and yet bordering on pleased.

"You know all my flaws and I know yours. There will be few surprises on those grounds. I enjoy your company more than nearly anyone else's—"

"Even outspoken as I am? I will not be returning to my soft-spoken guise not for anyone, even you." Her flashing green eyes dared him to find fault.

"I relish this bit of fire that you have donned. Not the vengeful bit that was flaunting your rebellion to your mother, but the genuine spark in you—yes, I like that very much. It is the woman you always were in your letters. At least, I am certain I shall never be bored with her. I feel very comfortable that I know her."

"I think you are the only one." Botheration—she was still not taking him seriously.

"Indeed. And I possess one more irresistible quality."

"Do tell me what that might be."

"You always said you would never marry a man of whom your mother approved. We both know, she has never thought well of a match between the two of us. My fortune is not equal to it."

A broad smile lit her face, and she laughed with every part of her being. "And that is your irresistible quality?"

"Can you deny that you find it appealing?" He flashed his eyebrows.

"Not nearly as appealing as so many other things about you." She pressed her hand to his cheek and leaned close to whisper, "But you are right, that might be the deciding factor."

He doubled over, the laughter welling in his belly

too much to contain. There would indeed never be a dull moment with her. "Then you accept my offer?"

Her eyes shimmered, but this time there was joy in them. "I do."

Slowly, carefully, he cupped her face in his broad hands and pulled her to him. How warm and soft and welcoming her lips! She wrapped her arms around his waist and pressed close, so very close.

"Have you any idea how tempting you are, woman?"

"I was hoping for that effect."

"Minx, of course you were." He kissed her again firmly. "And as tempting as it is, you cannot miss the ball in favor of other distractions. Pray, will you allow me to escort you?"

"Only if you promise to dance enough dances with me to make everyone wonder what is about."

"On any other night I would, very happily. But, it is Georgiana's night, I cannot do that. Nothing should distract from her. I have promised her a set, but I will dance the supper set and the last set with you, and will dance with no one else tonight. Will that do?"

"I suppose it will have to. As long as those two—"

"Friends of Mrs. Darcy?"

"Yes, them." Her nosed wrinkled as she sniffed, not unlike her mother's. "As long as you do not dance with them, I shall be content."

"And well-behaved?"

"I promise you shall have no reason to ask that of me ever again."

He kissed her forehead. "Somehow I doubt that."

"Vexing, contrary man."

"Always, my dearest. Always."

He escorted her downstairs, music wafting up the stairs from the ballroom. Had that conversation truly just happened? No approving crowd awaited their arrival. Somehow, after what had transpired, it seemed there should be. But it would be just as well. There would be plenty of attention when Aunt Catherine had her share of the conversation.

That probably should bother him. But it did not. Too many other pleasant feelings bubbled about within for there to be room for anything dismal or dreary.

"Elizabeth has turned the ballroom into a true fairyland," Anne whispered. Something in her eyes suggested she felt the same as he.

"This night will be talked about for years to come."

"I hope what you see meets your approval." Elizabeth appeared behind them. "It is good to see you, Anne. I had feared, for a moment, you would not be joining us."

"I feared the same thing for just a little while. But Fitzwilliam made me see things a little differently." She winked at him saucily.

Elizabeth's eyebrows rose high, and she glanced at Fitzwilliam. He grinned, obvious to be sure, but how was a newly betrothed man to behave?

"The musicians are excellent tonight. I look forward to dancing." Anne peered into the dancers, probably looking for the 'two ninnies' as she called them.

"I hope you shall enjoy the bonfire just before dinner, as well."

"Bonfire? I have never heard of such a thing." Anne had the good grace to look surprised.

"Good." Elizabeth smiled a little too broadly. It seemed she was enjoying the evening a very great deal already.

The musicians finished the set and the dancers faded off the floor. Moments later, servants appeared with trays of ices.

Anne disappeared for a moment and returned with two glasses. "Lemon. My favorite." She handed him one.

Georgiana rushed up to them. "I am so glad to see you! I asked for lemon ices just for you! You are so beautiful—it came out just as we imagined. Your drawings have done so much to set the scene. I am so very glad you came!" She caught Anne's free hand and squeezed it.

"Shall we have the next dance?" Fitzwilliam extended his hand.

"Oh, Fitzwilliam, I am so sorry, I know you asked for one, but I have promised every dance until dinner! Pray forgive me."

"This is your night, my dear, I am hardly offended. Dancing with your old cousin is not nearly as appealing as dancing with any of the young men in attendance. Dance with whomever you like." He patted her shoulder.

"Are you certain? I would not offend you for the world."

"I know. Go off and enjoy yourself."

"Thank you so much!" Georgiana was swept into a small group of young people and disappeared into the crowd.

He looked over his shoulder at Anne. "Shall we to the card room then, unless you seek to find another partner?"

"You cannot be rid of me so easily, sir. Will it be whist or commerce?"

"Whatever game you most prefer to lose."

They played through several hands of cards, until the supper set formed, and he escorted her back to the ballroom.

How intoxicating it was to dance with a woman whose eyes were only for him. She held him locked in a gaze that was at the same time powerful and painfully intimate and demanded nothing less from him. If anyone truly looked at them and saw—it would be utterly scandalous.

But in the press of the ballroom, it was unlikely.

They stepped together, turned, circled back to back, never breaking that bond. Each step, each breath in rhythm, connected by an invisible cord that somehow had always connected them.

Yes, it had always been that way. They may not have known it, but was it too sentimental to say their hearts had? Perhaps it was, but it did not make it less true. The way her eyes glittered—she felt it, she knew it, too.

The dance ended, and Darcy stepped into the center of the room, Elizabeth on his arm. "It is eleven thirty. As you know all the Christmastide greenery must be taken down and burned by midnight. Everyone, take a bit of evergreen and follow us outside for a bonfire and carols before supper."

Gasps and sounds of approval filled the room. That had never been done at Pemberley before. Was it something Elizabeth had done with her own family or was it something she and Darcy had contrived together? Whatever the reason, it was a delightful notion.

Darcy approached and leaned close. "Pray help everyone outside and direct the fire. I have a brief matter to attend to, and then I shall be there."

"Is everything all right?"

Darcy glanced at the doorway where Elizabeth stood, obviously waiting for him. "There are a few matters she wishes to discuss regarding the rest of the evening. It will only be a few minutes."

The look on Elizabeth's face did not suggest it was that small a matter, but it did not suggest anything wrong, either. "Very well, I am happy to assist my gracious host."

Darcy nodded and returned to his wife.

ELIZABETH TOOK DARCY'S arm and they proceeded downstairs to the small parlor at the front of the house. She took a candle from the hallway and lit several in the room, just enough to see by.

"Is there something wrong?" Darcy asked, his brows knitting. The small knot in his stomach wound in on itself.

"That is what you always ask. Why must you first assume that there is something wrong?" She touched his cheek. "Not to worry. Everything is fine."

"Then pray tell, if there is no crisis, why are we here, during the height of the ball?"

"I have a gift for you, one I have been waiting for some time to give to you." Her eyes twinkled in the conundrum that was Elizabeth.

"And now is the right time?"

"It was only a few minutes ago that I became certain it was absolutely the right time. It is Twelfth Night after all." She pressed her fingers to her lips and went to the chest of drawers in the corner. The top drawer was stuck, and she had to wrestle it open to remove a small package wrapped in white linen. "Here, this will answer all your questions."

The package was oddly shaped and lumpy, tied a bit awkwardly with a white ribbon. He untied it, and the linen fell away. "Where did you find this?" He held up the silver teething coral, its bells tinkling softly. He blew the whistle, its mellow sweet tone filled the small room. The family heirloom had been passed through at least three generations of Darcys, protecting them through that dangerous period of teething. It was said since its acquisition, no infant had died during that dreaded transition.

She looked at him, biting her lip.

"I have not seen this since—has it been that long? Since—Georgiana was a baby ..." he dropped the teething coral and its linen wrapper. As it hit the floor, the fabric revealed its true shape—a daintily embroidered baby dress. "You are—"

"Yes. I have suspected for some time, but only felt the quickening as we danced just now."

"So then you are well? All the tiredness, all the days you have felt poorly—"

"I am assured they are perfectly normal for a woman in my condition."

"Elizabeth!" He grabbed her by the waist and whirled her around. "Pray forgive me! I am sure I should not have done that."

She laughed clutching his arm for balance, the sound much like the silver bells. "It is fine, I assure you. I take it you are pleased?"

"I can think of no finer gift this Twelfth Night than to know our family is about to increase. You have made me the happiest of men."

"And I thought you already were."

"Teasing woman."

She might have replied, but it was exceedingly difficult when he was kissing her.

FITZWILLIAM THREW THE last of the evergreens on the bonfire and stepped back. He signaled the musicians who began to play *Hark the Herald Angels Sing*. The crowd circling the bonfire joined voices in the familiar carol.

Beside him, Anne sang. Her voice was really quite sweet—sweeter than her disposition, which really was not a bad thing. Too much sweetness could drive a man to boredom. Life with her would be anything but.

The bonfire snapped and crackled behind them, surrounding her in a frame of orange flame.

"You look like a phoenix rising up out of the fire you know," he whispered in her ear.

"In some ways, I think I am—we are both poised on an utterly new life."

"You may just be right. Certainly nothing will ever be the same again, will it?"

"No, it will not. Who knew that there was something to creaming the well after all?" She turned to him, eyebrow arched; so impertinent.

"What are you talking about?"

"Have you forgotten? You were the one who drank the first water from the well that morning—the water that I drew."

"So you attribute my proposal to that?" He leaned in very close and whispered, "And not to the very real fact that I love you?"

She gasped and gazed directly into his eyes. "You should not say such things."

"Why not, if they are true?"

"You have had too much punch."

"You have been with me the whole evening. I have had no punch." He took her hand, her long, cold fingers twining with his.

"You mean it?"

"I only hope that perhaps—"

She rose up on tiptoes, her breath tickling his ear. "I love you too, Fitzwilliam."

"Woman, if we were not in the middle of a crowd, I would kiss you." And he just might do so in any case—but for it being Georgiana's night.

"We will not be in the midst of a crowd all night."

"I am counting on that."

LATE THE FOLLOWING afternoon, Darcy, Elizabeth, Anne, and Fitzwilliam gathered in the small parlor. They had all been up until the very small hours and were only just now starting their day, still yawning and bleary-eyed. If Darcy had his druthers, they would have spent the whole day abed, but Fitzwilliam had said they all needed to talk. So here they were.

A nuncheon made up largely of food left from the ball had been set out on a low table in the center of a group of chairs. Elizabeth poured tea.

"Congratulations to you both, I cannot imagine happier news." Fitzwilliam clapped Darcy's shoulder.

Darcy leaned back in his chair, smiling. He had not been able to stop since Elizabeth's gift last night.

"I cannot believe you kept your suspicions to

yourself all this time." Anne accepted a teacup from Elizabeth. "How ever did you remain so tight-lipped? I think I would have revealed everything from the first moment I suspected something."

"This has been such a very eventful Christmastide, I hardly had time to breathe, much less think of a way to bring up the matter at all." Elizabeth blushed.

Not to mention that she desperately wanted to avoid Aunt Catherine's advice on the matter. That could motivate anyone to silence.

"It does explain all those things you have been fretting about though, Darcy. I am glad it is all explained so easily." Fitzwilliam heaped a plate with Twelfth Night pies. As many as were left in the kitchen, they might well be eating them until spring.

"As am I." Darcy leaned back and sipped his tea.

"I have some news as well." Anne glanced at Fitzwilliam.

Something about that look in her eyes—Darcy nearly dropped his teacup.

Anne sniggered.

"Do relax, Darce." Fitzwilliam uncrossed his legs and leaned forward.

"I will—once you have told me your news." Darcy knotted his hand around the arm of his chair. Knowing the two of them, they might have decided to take up ballooning together or something even more outlandish.

"I never knew I held such power over you, cousin."

"Stop teasing him, Anne. That is quite cruel." Fitzwilliam chortled. "Last night, we came to an understanding. Anne and I are to be married."

"Married?" Darcy nearly kicked the tea-table.

"I cannot say I am surprised." Elizabeth stirred a spoonful of sugar into her tea. "All the signs have been there for quite some time. You have been the best of friends for years."

"Do we have your support? Honestly, it does not matter if we do or do not, we shall marry. I would just prefer to have you behind us." Fitzwilliam popped the last bite of his pie into his mouth.

"Just tell me, this is what you want? This is not to spite Aunt Catherine or—"

"No need to list out all your suspicions, I can assure you, none of them are true." Fitzwilliam nodded at Anne who did likewise.

"And it is not just the impulse of the moment?"

"I am impulsive, I confess, but not that impulsive." Anne laughed lightly—it was a pleasing sound now that the bitterness was gone from it. "I—we are entirely certain—"

"Of what are you certain? How can you possibly be certain of anything without consulting with me first?" Aunt Catherine swooped in, waiting behind Darcy until he brought a chair near the table for her. "I am glad you are all here. It is imperative that I speak with you all."

Naturally, they had gathered here with absolutely nothing else in mind. Darcy pinched his temples.

"I do not like how you kept Anne to yourself last night, Fitzwilliam, that must stop immediately." Aunt Catherine rapped her knuckles on the table, rattling the teacups. "We must all come together and establish a plan for introducing Anne into wider society."

"No, I am not going to stop keeping her to myself." Fitzwilliam paused, clearly enjoying the slack-jaw expression on Aunt Catherine's face. "In fact, I intend to continue for the rest of my life."

"What are you blathering about? Do be serious."

"I am going to marry Anne."

"What nonsense. Stop joking and do be serious."

"I am entirely and completely serious." Considering the edge that sharpened Fitzwilliam's voice, she would do well to listen, but it was unlikely she would.

"I forbid it. You know I have for years. You are not at all a suitable match for her. I will not have you." She leaned back and crossed her arms as if that settled the matter.

"You do not have the right to make that decision, Mother." Anne's voice was soft and level—a little frightening in her severity.

"Whatever are you talking about? I am your mother. Of course I have the right."

"I am of age, and have been for some time, which I fear you have conveniently forgotten. It is my decision to make. You cannot stop me."

"Yes I can, I am your mother." Aunt Catherine rose slowly, like a kraken lingering from the previous night's fairyland.

"You can repeat yourself all that you want, but it does not matter. I can marry whomever I want."

"Darcy, tell her she cannot."

"We support Fitzwilliam and Anne."

"How can you do this to me?" Aunt Catherine's voice turned shrill and a little desperate. Did she realize she would ultimately lose this battle?

"What have you to do with any of this? I am the one to be married, not you. I am very fond of Fitzwilliam and can think of no one who will suit me better."

"And we agree with her." Elizabeth's tone was deceptively mild.

Aunt Catherine marched to Elizabeth, shouting over her, "Of course you would—you made out well for yourself pursuing an unsuitable match. You had no right to set your sights on Darcy, and now your vulgar influence is spreading to the rest of the family."

"Enough!" Darcy sprang to his feet, towering over Aunt Catherine.

Fitzwilliam jumped between them. "Do not get in the middle of this. This is my fight and I would thank you to keep your offense to yourself." He pushed Darcy back a step. "You think I am taking advantage of Anne?"

"Of course you are? What is your fortune?"

"You may want to reconsider disparaging the man who will be determining your style of living for the rest of your days, Lady Catherine." Elizabeth took a dainty bite from a Twelfth Night pie, not even looking up at the dispute swirling above her.

"If you do not offend him irreparably," Darcy returned to his seat, "you may find him to be the most sympathetic of any man to your cause. After all, his father might well take offense if his younger sister is not made comfortable. I know of no other with such a reason to be kind to you."

Aunt Catherine's expression changed into something he had never seen before, and she closed her mouth.

"I think perhaps we have a great deal to discuss. May we use your study?" Fitzwilliam helped Anne to her feet and took Aunt Catherine's arm.

Darcy watched them walk out and moved his chair closer to Elizabeth.

"I would say that is a propitious beginning." Her eyebrows rose into a fine arch.

"You would?"

"I would say that any beginning that rendered Lady Catherine speechless bodes well."

She looked so very serious as she spoke. Who could blame him for laughing heartily? "I am sorry. It appears that my family has once again intruded upon our Christmastide. But, as I am now out of aunts to interfere, perhaps next year we might rely upon your family to impose."

"My dearest, I know you are joking, but you must bear in mind, I still have two sisters unmarried. I expect they are entirely as capable of providing an interesting Christmastide as your aunts. But let us not count our chickens before they are hatched. Your sister is unmarried, too."

He groaned. "No more talk of unmarried sisters. Next Christmastide we will have a little one, a Christmastide blessing of our own. Let us dwell upon that."

"Indeed Mr. Darcy. Indeed we shall."

Author's Note

Newspapers, Gossip Columns and Scandal Mongers

It seems people have always been hungry for news. Not unlike today with abounding media outlets, newspapers proliferated during the Regency era. In spite of heavy taxation, high costs, and government censorship (that could include prosecution for libel!) by 1816, thirty one national newspapers were published in Britain, including fourteen in London itself. Some published daily, some several times a week, and some even less regularly. Daily papers included: *The Morning Chronicle, Morning Post, The Times,* and *The Morning Herald.* (Bolen, 2012)

Newspapers were not cheap. Costing around seven pence apiece (over half the price being tax!), they were often shared among many readers at coffee houses and circulating libraries or passed among friends and family members around the neighborhood.

The dawn of serious journalism

What did these popular papers publish? Most of those who (could afford to) read newspapers were interested in parliamentary proceedings. Consequently, reports on those often took up at least half the print space. (Day, 2006) The rest of the space—often in relatively haphazard order—was taken up by the rest of the news. Reports on the visual and performing arts became increasingly popular during the era. News of crime and punishments including bankruptcies, duels and seductions appeared with almost monotonous regularity. (Fullerton, 2004)

Some news was difficult to report, particularly that related to the Peninsula war. Captain Rees Howell Gronow noted, "there was a very limited and imperfect amount of intelligence which the best journals were enabled to place before their readers (the progress of the Peninsular campaign was very imperfectly chronicled.)" (Summerville, 2006) To answer some of this difficulty, *The Times of London* sent the first war correspondent, Henry Crabb Robinson, to Spain to report on the Peninsula War. (Grum, 1975) In contrast, Adm. Nelson did not leave the job to reporters. He ensured that he received praise and public recognition by issuing press releases to the papers directly. (Summerville, 2006)

Such a wide variety of sources suggests a wide range in the reliability of various newspapers. Indeed, some had high standards, publishing what we would consider today to be important news including new of Parliament, war correspondence, current events and even the weather. (Journalism standards and ethics were also being established during this period, which considering what some papers printed, was a very necessary thing.)

For example London's *The Examiner*, edited by the Hunt brothers, James Leigh and John, published serious news, even though it was not always popular. Among other things, they called the government to task for the heavy taxation. In 1812, they criticized the Prince Regent for gambling and womanizing and running up huge debts while not doing anything for the citizenry. Despite the truth of what they printed, the Hunts were sued for libel and James Leigh imprisoned for two years though he continued to edit *The Examiner* from prison. Gaston (2008)

...and not so serious

Other newspapers flourished by reporting the scandals of the "the celebrities of the day. Women of the peerage, like royalty, combined the glamour of present-day Hollywood with the power and prestige of modern political and economic elites. Aristocratic comings and goings, successes and failures, travels and travails, were avidly reported in the English press." (Lewis, 1986) Reports of elopements were frequently published under the heading 'Fashionable World.' Other missteps might find their way under columns dedicated to 'Fashionable Faux Pas.'

Even the ordinary news of a betrothal in the *Morning Post*, the *Gazette* or *The Times* could be spiced up by reporting the bride's fortune—whether the reporter knew the actual amount or not. Sometimes, the announcements did not give the name of the bride, only that of her father and any titled connections—

because of course that was what really of interest to readers. (Jones, 2009)

Reporters often purchased their juicy tidbits from servants less than loyal to their masters and gentlemen and ladies willing to expose their friends. Purchasing gossip could get expensive; blackmail was much cheaper. Some newspapers were known to take money to not print some embarrassing incident—which might or might not actually even be true. (Gaston, 2008)

One of the most notorious of such journalists was Theodore Hook. He lost a great deal of money in a government job when a clerk under him embezzled money he was responsible for. To make up for lost income, Hook started the Sunday newspaper, *The John Bull*.

Unlike the Hunts, he sided with the Prince Regent—not a bad idea considering his situation. In his paper, he freely criticized prominent Whigs and even Queen Caroline and her attendants. Even more endearing, while not above paying for gossip, Hook gleaned most of his information by keeping his identity as editor of *The John Bull* a secret, and essentially spying on his friends and connections. Charming guy, huh? (Gaston, 2008)

Away from London, country newspapers reported on the doings of the local landowners—the closest thing passing for a celebrity in the remote regions. Local gentry would then include these scintillating tidbits in their letter so local news did not stay local very long. Sufficiently scandalous items managed to find their way into the national papers.

Even with the use of initials and dashes to substitute for full names (ostensibly to protected editors from legal actions) little remained private. When things were especially salacious full names were often used citing the 'concern for public morality.' (Jones, 2009) Crim con trials were a particular favorite scandal to report on.

Crim con trials

Crim con trials, or more properly Criminal Conversation trials, were the part of a divorce proceeding where a wife's infidelity was proven in a court of law. Since divorce required a literal act of Parliament, only the very wealthy and well-connected were able to even consider seeking a divorce, effectively guaranteeing that crim con trials would be newsworthy.

The trials tended to be colorful, highly publicized events open to the general public—as close to modern reality TV as the Regency era could get. For those not fortunate enough to be able to attend in person, most book sellers carried newspaper, pamphlets, transcripts and 'true' exposés documenting all the sexual misadventures of high society.

Barristers on both sides of the case played up the drama as much for the public notoriety as for the effect on the court's decisions. During the 1809 Clarke scandal, the Duke of York bore the humiliation of having his love letters to Mrs. Clarke read out to the entire House of Commons and published in every scandal seeking newspaper in the country.

Trial proceedings called upon servants, especially young pretty ones, to deliver testimony for both the plaintiff and the defense. While servants could be (mostly) excused for presenting sensational tales in coarse language, the barristers were gentlemen and adopted notably euphemistic and flowery language to express the necessary elements with decency and taste. Some said it became something of an art form.

With so much at stake, both in terms of finances and reputations, truth and accuracy fell to the need to convince jurors. What better fodder for sensation hungry editors to use to sell newspapers? Not surprisingly, the papers sold out as fast as they could be printed. (Murray, 1998)

Of course, all this sounds nothing like the media today, does it? One more case of the more things change, the more they stay the same.

References

Bolen, Cheryl. The Proliferation of Newspapers in Regency England." The Beau Monde. March 22. 2012. Nov. 27, 2017 .http://thebeaumonde.com/the-proliferation-of-newspapers-in-regency-england/

Fullerton, Susannah. *Jane Austen and Crime*. Sydney: Jane Austen Society of Australia, 2004.

Gaston, Diane. "Scandal! Gossip! Research." Risky Regencies. August 25, 2008. Accessed Nov. 27, 2017   .
http://www.riskyregencies.com/2008/08/25/scandal-gossip-research/

Gronow, R. H., and C. J. Summerville. *Regency Recollections: Captain Gronow's Guide to Life in London and Paris*. Welwyn Garden City, U.K.: Ravenhall, 2006.

Grun, Bernard. *The timetables of history: a chronology of world events: based on Werner Steins "Kulturfahrplan"*. London: Thames and Hudson, 1975.

Harvey, A. D. Sex in Georgian England: Attitudes

and Prejudices from the 1720s to the 1820s. New York: St. Martin's Press, 1994.

Jones, Hazel. *Jane Austen and Marriage*. London: Continuum, 2009.

Lewis, Judith Schneid. *In the Family Way: Childbearing in the British Aristocracy, 1760-1860*. New Brunswick, N.J.: Rutgers University Press, 1986.

Murray, Venetia. An Elegant Madness: High Society in Regency England. New York: Viking, 1999.

Wilkes, Roger. *Scandal: a scurrilous history of gossip*. London: Atlantic, 2003.

Acknowledgments

So many people have helped me along the journey taking this from an idea to a reality.

Anji, Julie, and Debbie thank you so much for cold reading, proof reading and being honest!

And my dear friend Cathy, my biggest cheerleader, you have kept me from chickening out more than once!

And my sweet sister Gerri who believed in even those first attempts that now live in the file drawer!

Thank you!

✣Other Books by Maria Grace

Remember the Past
The Darcy Brothers

Given Good Principles Series:

Darcy's Decision
The Future Mrs. Darcy
All the Appearance of Goodness
Twelfth Night at Longbourn

Jane Austen's Dragons Series:

Pemberley: Mr. Darcy's Dragon
Longbourn: Dragon Entail

The Queen of Rosings Park Series:

Mistaking Her Character
The Trouble to Check Her
A Less Agreeable Man

Sweet Tea Stories:

A Spot of Sweet Tea: Hopes and Beginnings (short story anthology)
A Spot of Sweet Tea: Hopes and Beginnings: Christmastide tales (Christmas novella anthology)

Darcy & Elizabeth: Chrismas 1811
The Darcy's First Christmas

From Admiration to Love
Snowbound at Hartfield

Regency Life (Nonfiction) Series:

A Jane Austen Christmas: Regency Christmas Traditions
Courtship and Marriage in Jane Austen's World

Short Stories:

Four Days in April
Sweet Ginger
Last Dance
Not Romantic

Available in paperback, e-book, and audiobook format at all online bookstores.

On Line Exclusives at:

About the Author

Though Maria Grace has been writing fiction since she was ten years old, those early efforts happily reside in a file drawer and are unlikely to see the light of day again, for which many are grateful. After penning five file-drawer novels in high school, she took a break from writing to pursue college and earn her doctorate in Educational Psychology. After 16 years of university teaching, she returned to her first love, fiction writing.

She has one husband and one grandson, two graduate degrees and two black belts, three sons, four undergraduate majors, five nieces, is starting her sixth year blogging on Random Bits of Fascination, has built seven websites, attended eight English country dance balls, sewn nine Regency era costumes, and shared her life with ten cats.

She can be contacted at:

author.MariaGrace@gmail.com

Facebook:
http://facebook.com/AuthorMariaGrace

On Amazon.com:
http://amazon.com/author/mariagrace

Random Bits of Fascination
(http://RandomBitsofFascination.com)

Austen Variations (http://AustenVariations.com)

English Historical Fiction Authors
 (http://EnglshHistoryAuthors.blogspot.com)

White Soup Press (http://whitesouppress.com/)

On Twitter @WriteMariaGrace

On Pinterest: http://pinterest.com/mariagrace423/

Made in United States
North Haven, CT
28 December 2022

30266688R00119